THE FURTHER ADVENTURES OF

THE
COWDOG®

D0956191

Illustrations by Gerald L. Holmes

Maverick Books
Published by Gulf Publishing Company
Houston, Texas

To my children,
Scot, Ashley, and Mark

Maverick Books
Published by Gulf Publishing Company
P.O. Box 2608 Houston, Texas 77252-2608

10   9   8   7   6   5   4

Library of Congress Cataloging-in-Publication Data
Erickson, John R., 1943–
    The further adventures of Hank the Cowdog/John R.
Erickson.
        p. cm.
    Summary: Hank the Cowdog almost loses his job as Head of
Ranch Security when he develops a case of Eye-Crosserosis.
    ISBN 0-87719-117-4 (pbk.)
    ISBN 0-87719-120-4 (cl.)
    ISBN 0-87719-122-0 (cassette)
    1. Dogs—Fiction. [1. Dogs—Fiction. 2. Humorous
stories.   3. West (U.S.)—Fiction.] I. Title.
PS3555.R428F87   1990
813'.54—dc20
[Fic]
                                              90-6655
                                                 CIP

Book and cover design by Tom Hair.

Printed in the United States of America.

Hank the Cowdog is a registered trademark
of John R. Erickson.

CONTENTS

Have you read all of Hank's adventures?
Available in paperback at $6.95:

All books are available on audio cassette too!
($15.95 for two cassettes)

Also available on cassettes:
Hank the Cowdog's Greatest Hits!

CHAPTER

1

THE SILVER PERIL

I t's me again, Hank the Cowdog. As I recall, it was the 14th of May when the silver monster bird swooped down on the ranch and threatened us with death and destruction.

Or was it May 15th? Could have been the 16th. Anyway . . .

Silver monster birds are huge creatures with a body that's long and skinny, resembles the body of a snake, which makes me think they might be a cross-breed between a bird and a reptile. The head sort of confirms that, because it has a sharp nose and two wicked eyes.

In other words, it ain't your usual bird head. Oh yes, did I mention that they don't have a beak? No beak whatsoever. That's a pretty important clue right there. It ain't natural. Show

1

me a bird without a beak and I've got some questions to ask him.

Another thing about the silver monster birds is that they have shiny feathers—not your usual dull brown or glossy black, but bright, shiny silver feathers. And a lot of the monster birds will have a white marking on the side which resembles a star.

They have big drooping wings with several things growing out of the under side. I call them "things" because I don't have a technical term for them yet. Whatever they are, starlings and blackbirds and sparrows don't have them. They may be poison stingers, I don't know.

These silver monster birds don't flap their wings. They glide like a buzzard or a hawk. And did I mention that they roar? Yes sir, they roar, and I mean LOUD. Your ordinary bird doesn't do that. He might cheep or squawk or sing a little tune, but you very rarely find one that roars.

It's the roar that makes the silver monster birds a little scary. It takes a special kind of dog to stand up to that roar, hold his ground, and keep on barking. I suspect that even some cowdogs would run from that terrible sound, but on this ranch we don't run *from* danger. We run *to* it.

Anyway, one day last week I caught a silver monster bird trying to slip onto the ranch. He should have known he couldn't get away with it. I mean, that roar is a dead give-away. My ears are very sensitive to certain sounds and there aren't too many roars that get past me.

Drover and I had put in a long night patrolling headquarters, fairly routine, as I recall. About the only excitement came a little after midnight when Drover got into a scuffle with a cricket. I told him to save his energy for bigger stuff. I mean, crickets cause a certain amount of damage around the place, but they ain't what you'd call a major threat.

I figger Pete can handle the cricket department and we'll take care of the more dangerous assignments. Course the problem with that is that Pete won't do it. Too lazy. He's a typical cat, but I don't want to get started on cats.

Anyway, Drover and I came in from night patrol and bedded down under the gas tanks. I scratched around on my gunny sack and got it fluffed up just right and had curled up for a long nap, when all at once I heard it.

My right ear went up. My ears are highly trained, don't you see, and they sort of have a mind of their own. I can be dead asleep and lost in beautiful dreams, but those ears never

sleep. They never go off duty. (This is fairly typical of your blue-ribbon, top-of-the-line cowdogs.)

I suppose I was dreaming about Beulah again. Derned woman is hard to get off my mind. I don't let women distract me during working hours, but sometimes I lose control when I'm asleep. I mean, a guy can keep an iron grip on himself only so long. Every once in a while he kind of goes to seed.

Well, I heard the roar. My right ear went up. My left ear went up. I glanced around. "Beulah?"

My sawed-off, short-haired, stub-tailed assistant lifted his head and stared at me. "I'm not Beulah. I'm Drover."

I studied the runt for a second, and my head began to clear. "I know who you are."

"How come you called me Beulah?"

"I didn't."

"I'm almost sure you did."

"Drover, *almost sure* might be close enough for some lines of work, but in the security business you have to be positive. You need to work on that."

"Okay, Hank."

"Now, what's that noise?"

Drover looked up in the trees and rolled his eyes. "I don't hear any . . ." And right then he heard the roar. His eyes got as big as saucers and he started to shiver. "What is it, Hank?"

"I don't know, but we're fixing to find out. I've got a hunch that it's a silver monster bird."

I turned my head just for a second, and when I looked back, Drover was gone. At first I thought he might have headed for the machine shed, but then I saw his gunny sack quivering.

"Get out from under there! We've got work to do. I'm putting this ranch under Red Alert."

"But Hank, that thing roars!"

The roar was getting louder all the time. "Come on, son, it's time for battle stations. If that bird lands, it's liable to be a fight to the death."

"But Hank, I . . . my foot hurts and I got a headache."

I took a corner of his gunny sack in my teeth and jerked it away. And there was Drover, my assistant Head of Ranch Security, quivering like a tub full of raw liver. "Get up and stay behind me. This ain't drill. This is Red Alert."

"Okay, Hank, I'll try but . . . Red Alert's pretty serious, isn't it . . . oh, my foot hurts!"

I took the lead and went streaking out into the pasture south of the house. I headed straight to the big dead cottonwood between the house and the creek and set up a forward position. I could see him now, coming in low over the hills and heading straight toward us.

It was a silver monster bird, all right, one of the biggest I'd ever seen. He had his big droopy wings out and his eyes were going back and forth across the ground. He was looking for something to swoop down on and kill. I could see that right off. I mean, if you've seen as many of these monster birds as I have, you sort of learn to read their thoughts.

This one had murder on his mind.

"Okay, Drover, listen up. I don't want to repeat myself. We've got steers in this home pasture. That's what the monster bird's after, them steers. He's gonna try to swoop down and pick up a steer and fly off with him."

Drover's teeth were chattering. "A whole steer!"

"Yes sir. They dive down and snatch 'em up and eat 'em in the air, and I mean bones and hair and teeth, ears, tail, everything. It's our job to keep him from doing that."

"What would he do . . . if he caught a dog instead of a steer?"

"We don't have an answer to that question."

"I . . . I'd kind of like to know before we do anything radical."

"Use your imagination."

"My leg hurts, Hank. I think I better . . ."

"Stand your ground and listen. When I count to three, we'll go over the top and let him have it. Don't save anything back. If he comes in low enough, we'll try to grab him."

"*Grab him!* But Hank, what would we do with him?"

I studied on that for a second. I hadn't thought that far ahead. "I guess just bite and scratch and fight for your life. You ready?"

"No."

"Well, ready or not, this is it—combat, Red Alert." I peeked over the top of the log. He was heading straight toward us.

"Oh my gosh, Hank, look how big he is, and his eyes, and his wings are smoking!"

"One!"

"Hank, my leg . . ."

"Two!"

". . . is killing me."

"Three! Attack, Drover! Charge! Bonzai!"

I leaped over the dead tree and threw myself into the monster bird's path. It was him or me. I bared my fangs and set up a ferocious bark, probably the ferociousest bark I ever made.

The roar was deafening. I mean, it shook the ground. Never heard anything quite so loud or frightful in all my career. No ordinary dog could have stood his ground against that thing.

He kept coming, so I leaped into the air and snapped at him. Another foot or two and I might have put a fang-lock on him, but when he saw my teeth coming at him, he made the only sensible decision and quit the country.

I mean, he pointed himself north and evacuated, and he never looked back. The smoke and roar faded into the distance.

"And don't you ever try that again!" I yelled at him as he went past. "Next time, you won't get off so easy."

I turned to Drover. He was lying flat on the ground with his paws over his ears. His eyes were shut tight. He wouldn't get no medals for bravery, but at least he hadn't run.

"Okay, Drover, you can come out now."

"Are we dead?"

"Nope. Against near impossible odds, we just whipped a silver monster bird."

Drover cracked his eyes, looked around in a full circle, and sat up. "How bad was it?"

"How bad? Almost beyond description, Drover. When he had me in his claws . . ."

"He had you in his claws, no fooling?"

"You didn't see it? Yup, he had these enormous claws with big hooks on the end, and he reached down and grabbed me."

"What did you do?"

"What did I do? Well, I called on an old trick that my granddaddy once told me about. I tore

9

off his whole leg and left him with a bloody stump.''

"You did?''

"Certainly did. Why do you think he flew away in such a hurry? I mean, that bird was scared when he left out of here, and I have my doubts that we'll ever see him again.''

Drover looked around. "Where's the leg?''

"Oh, it's around here somewhere. We'll run into it one of these days. Can't miss it. Heck, it was almost as big as this tree.''

"You want me to look for it?''

"Not now. I don't know about you, Drover, but I'm ready to shower out and shut her down for a few hours. I think we've earned ourselves some sleep.''

And with that, we headed for our favorite spot on the ranch, the place just west of the house where the septic tank overflows and forms a beautiful pool of green water.

CHAPTER
2

EGGED ON BY PETE

In the security business, you learn to live your life a day at a time because you never know if you'll make it past that next monster. Any one of them is liable to be your last.

A lot of dogs can't handle that kind of pressure, but there's others of us who kind of thrive on danger. When you're in that category, you learn to savor the precious moments. I mean the little things that most dogs take for granted.

Like a roll in the sewer after a big battle. There's nothing quite like it, believe me. You come in hot and bloody and tore up and wore out, proud of yourself on the one hand but just derned near exhausted on the other hand, and you walk up to that pool of lovely green water

11

and . . . well, it's hard to describe the wonderfulness of it.

That first plunge is probably the best, when you step in and plop down and feel the water moving over your body. Then you roll around and kick your legs in the air and let your nose feast on that deep manly aroma.

Your poodles and your chihuahuas and your other varieties of house dogs never know the savage delight of a good ranch bath. If they ever found what they're missing, they'd never be the same again. There's just something about it that makes a dog proud to be a dog.

Well, I climbed out of the sewer and shook myself and sat down in the warm sunshine. Drover was still standing in water up to his knees. I noticed that he hadn't rolled around in it. He never does. He just wades in and stands there, looking stiff and uncomfortable.

"How do you expect to get clean if you don't get yourself wet?"

He wrinkled his nose. "I don't like to get wet."

"This water has special power, son. It revives the spirit."

He kind of dipped down and got his brisket wet and scampered out on dry land. "There. I feel much better now."

I just shook my head. Sometimes Drover acts more like a cat than a cowdog. Makes me wonder . . . oh well.

We sunned ourselves for a few minutes, then headed on down to the gas tanks. I had a gunny sack bed down there with my name on it and I was all set to pour myself into it. I was fluffing it up again and getting it arranged just right when I heard the back door slam up at the house.

I perked my ears and listened. When the back door slams at that hour of the morning, it often means that Sally May has busted the yoke on Loper's breakfast egg. He won't eat busted eggs, for reasons which I don't understand. Seems to me that an egg's an egg, and after a guy chews it up and swallers it, it's all about the same anyway.

But Loper doesn't see it that way, which is fine with me because around here, in Co-op dog food country, an egg in any form is a gourmet delight.

I cut my eyes toward Drover. He had his chin resting on his front paws and was drifting off to sleep. He hadn't heard the door slam, and I didn't see that it was my duty to tell him about it.

I slipped away from the gas tanks and loped

up the hill. Had my taste buds all tuned up for a fried egg when I met Pete. He was going the same direction I was.

"Get lost, cat. Nobody called your name."

He gave me a hateful look and hissed. Well, you know me. I try to live by the Golden Rule: "Do unto others but don't take trash off the cats." Pete was in the market for a whipping, seemed to me, so I obliged him. Figgered I might as well get it over with, while it was fresh on both our minds.

I jumped him, rolled him, buried him, cuffed him a couple of times, and generally gave him a stern warning about how cats are supposed to behave. After I'd settled that little matter, I trotted up to the yard gate, ready for my egg.

Sally May was standing there with her hands on her hips. I sat down and swept the ground with my tail, gave her a big smile and sat up on my back legs.

I picked up this little begging trick some years ago. It was pretty tough to learn—I mean, it takes balance and coordination and considerable athletic ability—but it's paid off more than once. People seem to love it. They like to see a dog beg for what they're going to give him anyway. Don't ask me why, but they do.

Begging sort of goes against my grain. I mean, my ma was no ordinary mutt. She had papers and everything and cowdog pride was sort of bred into me. But a guy has to make a living, and now and then he finds himself cutting a few corners.

Well, I went up on my hind legs. Sometimes I get my balance the first time and sometimes I don't. This time it worked. I balanced myself on two legs, and then to add a special touch, I wagged my tail and moved my front paws at the same time.

I don't believe the trick could have been done any better. It was a real smasher.

I was so busy with the trick that I didn't notice the sour look on Sally May's face. "Hank, you big bully! You ought to be ashamed of yourself for picking on that poor cat!"

HUH?

"Just for that, you don't get this egg. Here, Pete, kitty, kitty, kitty."

In a flash, Pete was there. I mean, when it comes to free-loading, he has amazing speed. He gave me a surly grin and went through the gate and started eating my egg. That really hurt.

Sally May gave Kitty-Kitty a nice motherly smile, then she turned a cold glare on me. "And besides being a bully, you smell *awful.*"

How could she say that? I had just taken a bath, shampooed, the whole nine yards. I mean, a guy can't spend his whole life taking a bath. He's got to get out sometime, and when he does it's just natural that he picks up a few of the smells of the earth.

Besides that, I knew for a fact that Pete hadn't taken a bath in *years*. He hated water even more than Drover did. And he had dandruff too. You could see it all over him, looked like he'd been in a snowstorm.

What kind of justice do you have when a dog that takes a bath every day, and sometimes two or three times a day, gets accused of smelling bad, and a rinky-dink cat . . . oh well.

Pete was chewing my egg, and every now and then he'd turn his eyes toward me and give me a grin. Let me tell you, it took tremendous self-discipline for me to sit there and watch, when all of my savage instincts were urging me to tear down the fence and pulverize the cat.

Sally May went back into the house. I should have left right there, just walked away and tried to forget the whole thing. But I didn't.

Pete had laid down in front of the plate. I mean, he was too lazy to stand up and eat. He was purring and flicking the end of his tail back and forth and chewing every bite twenty-three times.

I found myself growling, just couldn't help

it. His head came up. "Hmmm, you hungry, Hankie? You'd like this egg. It just melts in your mouth."

"No thanks, I got better things to do." That was the truth. I did. But I stayed there.

Pete shrugged and went on eating. I watched, and before I knew it, I was drooling at the mouth.

Pete got up, took a big stretch, and ambled over to where I was. He started rubbing against the fence. He was so close, I could have snatched him baldheaded, which I wanted to do very sincerely, only there was a wire fence between us.

"I'm not sure I can eat all that egg," he said. "I'm stuffed. You want the rest of it, Hankie?"

I should have said no. I mean, a guy has his pride and everything. But my mouth went to watering at the thought of that egg and . . . "Oh, I might . . . yeah, I'll take it."

He grinned and ambled back to the plate. He picked up the egg in his mouth and brought it over to the fence and dropped it right in front of my nose.

Well, I wasn't going to give him a chance to reconsider, so I made a grab for it. Hit the derned fence with the end of my nose.

But it was right there in front of me. I mean,

I could smell it now, it was so close. It was giving off warm waves and delicious smells. I could even smell the butter it had been cooked in.

I made another snap at it, hit the fence and scabbed up my nose. Made my eyes water. When my vision cleared up, I saw Pete sitting there and grinning. I was losing patience fast.

"Gimme that egg. You said I could have it."

"Here, I'll move it a little closer." He got his nose under the egg and nudged it right against the fence.

Well, I just *knew* I could get it now, so I made another lunge for it. Got a taste of it this time, but also wrecked my nose on that frazzling wire. I could see a piece of skin sticking up, right out toward the end.

"Gimme that egg!"

He licked his paw and purred.

Okay, that settled it. I'll fool around and nickle-and-dime a problem for a while, but there comes a time when you've got to get down to brute strength.

I backed off and took a run at it and hit the fence with all my speed and strength. I expected at least two posts to snap off at the ground, and it wouldn't have surprised me if I had taken out the whole west side.

Them posts turned out to be a little stouter than I thought, and you might say that the wire didn't break either. The collision shortened my backbone by about six inches and also came close to ruining my nose.

"Gimme that egg, cat, or I'll . . ."

Pete throwed a hump into his back and hissed, right in my face. That was a serious mistake. No cat does that to Hank the Cowdog and lives to tell about it.

I started barking. I snarled, I snapped, I tore at the fence with my front paws, I clawed the ground. I mean, we had us a little riot going, fellers, and it was only a matter of time until Pete died a horrible death.

And through it all, I could still smell that egg, fried in butter.

The back door flew open and Loper stormed out. He had shaving cream on one side of his face and the other side was bright red.

"HANK, SHUT UP! YOU'RE GONNA WAKE UP THE BABY!"

I stopped barking and stared at him. Me? What had I . . . if it hadn't been for the cat . . .

I heard the baby squall inside the house. Sally May exploded out the door. "Will you tell your dog to shut up! He just woke the baby."

"Shut up, Hank!"

Shut up, Hank. Shut up, Hank. That's all anybody ever says to me. Not "good morning, Hank," or "thanks for saving the ranch from the silver monster bird, Hank, we really appreciate you risking your life while we were asleep." Nothing like that, no siree.

Well, I can take a hint. I gave Pete one last glare, just to let him know that his days on this earth were numbered, and I stalked back to the gas tanks.

I met Drover halfway down the hill. He'd just pried himself out of bed. "What's going on, Hank? I heard some noise."

I glared at him. "You heard some noise? Well, glory be. It's kind of a shame you didn't come a little sooner when you might have made a hand."

"You need some help?"

I glanced back up the hill. Sally May was still out in the yard, talking to her Kitty-Kitty. "Yeah, I need some help. Go up there and bark at the cat."

"Just . . . just bark at the cat, that's all?"

"That's all. Give it your best shot."

"Any special reason?"

"General principles, Drover."

"Well, okay. I'll see what I can do."

He went skipping up the hill and I went down to the gas tanks to watch the show.

Maybe it was kind of mean, me sending Drover up there on a suicide mission, when he was too dumb to know better. But look at it this way: I get blamed for everything around here, and most of the time I don't deserve it. I figgered it wouldn't hurt Drover to get yelled at once or twice, and it might even do him some good.

Getting yelled at is no fun, but it does build character. Drover needed some character-building. That was one of his mainest problems, a weak character.

So I watched. The little runt padded up to the fence, plopped down, sat up on his back legs, and started yipping. Sally May put her hands on her hips, gave her head a shake, and said, "Well, if that isn't the cutest thing!"

She pitched him my egg and he caught it in the air and gulped it down.

A minute later, he was down at the gas tanks. "I did what you said, Hank, and I won a free egg. Are you proud of me?"

I was so proud of him, I thought about blacking both his eyes. But I was too disgusted. I just went to sleep.

That seems to be the only thing I can do around here without getting yelled at: sleep.

CHAPTER

3

STRICKEN WITH EYE-CROSSEROSIS

I slept until late morning, maybe ten o'clock or so. What woke me up was Drover's wheezing.

He wheezes in his sleep, don't you see, and makes a very peculiar sound. Sometimes I can sleep through it and sometimes I can't. As a general rule, I'm a light sleeper. That's one of the prices you pay for having sensitive ears. You hear every sound in the night, including some you'd rather not.

Don't know what causes Drover's problem. He claims he's allergic to certain weeds. Maybe so. He's also allergic to hard work and danger in any form. Anyhow, there's definitely something wrong with his nose.

And speaking of noses, mine was in poor shape after that tussle with Pete and the wire fence. The black leathery part was all scraped up. By crossing my eyes like this . . . well, you can't see—by crossing my eyes I could sight down my nose and see the little flaps of skin rolled up.

I studied the damage for a long time. Kind of made me sad to see my old nose banged up that way. It's a well-known fact that a cowdog tends to be a little vain about his nose.

On the one hand it's a very delicate piece of equipment. On the other hand it's an object of beauty. Entire books have been written about the natural beauty of a cowdog's nose—or if they haven't been written, they ought to be. I bet they'd sell millions of copies and make somebody tubs full of money.

They used to tell that my Uncle Beanie packed his nose in mud every night. He lived to a ripe old age, and right up to the last the women were just nuts about him. He said it was his nose, said the mud treatment kept it soft and pretty.

Anyway, I sat there looking at my nose and listening to Drover wheeze and had my eyes crossed for a long time. And you know what?

G.L. Holmes

They got hung up—my eyes, I mean. I couldn't get them uncrossed. It's a serious condition called Eye-Crosserosis.

Kind of throwed a scare into me. I shook my head and tossed it up and down. Didn't help, eyes stayed crossed. I hit the side of my head with my left paw and that didn't help, so I scratched at it with my hind leg. Nuthin. I was getting a little concerned by this time, because my eyes being crossed throwed everything out of focus, don't you see, which sort of left the ranch defenseless.

Ma used to tell us not to cross our eyes when we were pups, said they might not go back to normal. I never believed her, but she was right.

Well, I finally decided I'd better sound the alarm. "Drover, wake up, we're in a world of trouble." He wheezed and snored, didn't wake up. "Drover! Get up, son, this is no time to sleep. We could be on the brink of a disaster."

His head came up and he opened his eyes. "Beulah?"

"Beulah!"

He blinked a couple of times. "You're not Beulah."

"I'm certainly not, and what do you mean, dreaming about *my* woman? You got no right . . . look at me, Drover, and tell me what you see."

He studied me for a long time, squinted one eye and then the other, looked me up one side and down the other.

"Well, what do you see? Go ahead and say it, just spit it out."

"A dog."

"Look deeper. Details."

He looked deeper. "A cowdog?"

"The face, Drover, study the face."

He cocked his head. "Oh yeah, I see it now. It looks terrible, Hank."

"I was afraid of that. It's pretty obvious, huh?"

"Sure is."

"Do you think I look disfigured? I mean, I don't want to go around looking like a loon or a freak or something."

"I'd say you look kind of disfigured, Hank."

That was discouraging news. I tried walking around and ran into one of the legs on the gas tanks. "The worst part of it is that it's messed up my vision. Can't see worth a rip."

"Huh. That's really strange, Hank. I wouldn't have thought it would do that."

"Oh, it's not so strange, when you think about it. What do you reckon I ought to do to cure it?"

"Beats me. Maybe a mud pack would help."

When a guy can't see, he'll try most anything. I followed Drover down to the sewer and he helped me up to the edge of the water. I dug balls of mud with my paws and plastered them over both eyes. Then I laid down to let the healing set in.

Must have laid there for half an hour. "What

do you think now, Drover? Have we waited long enough?"

"Well . . . it still looks the same to me. Maybe you better go another hour."

"Maybe so." About fifteen minutes later, I began to think about what he'd said. "Wait a minute. What do you mean, it still *looks* the same?" I heard him snore and wheeze. "Drover, wake up! What do you mean, it still looks the same to you?"

"Huh, what? What do I mean? Well, I guess that means it don't look any different."

"What are you talking about?"

"Your nose. It still looks beat-up and scabby to me."

"My nose! I wasn't talking about my nose, you little dunce."

"Oh."

"How could a scabby nose have anything to do with my vision?"

"I wondered about that."

I scraped off the mud and opened my eyes. I saw two Drovers staring at me. "It didn't help. I'm still afflicted."

"Hey! Your eyes are crossed!"

"Very good, Drover. It only took you . . . what, forty-five minutes to pick that up?"

"More like an hour."

"That's just great." I tried to think through my problem, one step at a time. "Well, this is a fine mess. What am I going to do now?"

"Well . . . if your eyes are crossed, maybe you could uncross 'em."

"What a wonderful idea, Drover."

"Yeah, it just came to me in a flash."

"I bet that was quite a flash."

"It was pretty good."

"Well, here's another flash. I already thought about that."

"You did?"

"And I tried it."

"You did?"

"And it didn't work."

"Oh."

"So do you have other flashes? I mean, with my eyes out of commission, this ranch is in real danger. If the coyotes ever got wind of this, we'd be almost helpless."

"Well . . . my eyes are pretty good. Maybe we could use my eyes and your judgment. How does that sound?"

I thought about that for a long time. I didn't want to rush into anything. Making cold, hard decisions is a very important part of being Head of Ranch Security. A guy just doesn't leap into those kinds of decisions.

"Maybe so. It may be our best shot. But remember: you're still working for me."

"Okay."

"You furnish the eyes and I'll furnish the brains, and . . ."

I stopped in the middle of the sentence. My left ear shot up. A pickup had just pulled in at the mailbox and was coming toward headquarters.

My reaction was completely automatic. I set up a bark and moved toward the sound and ran into Loper's roping dummy.

"Who is it, Drover, where are they, point me toward them, this could be serious stuff, *bark for Pete's sake,* sound the alarm!"

He let out his usual yip-yip-yip, which wouldn't have scared a fly, but I guess it was his best lick. "Okay, Hankie, follow me, here we go!"

Made me mighty uneasy, following Drover, but I didn't have much choice. We went tearing down the hill, me barking and Drover yipping. I kept right on his tail. I could see that much, even though it was double and out of focus.

All at once he came to a halt. I got myself shut down just in time, almost plowed him under. I mean, you get that much bulk and muscle going in high gear and you don't just stop on a dime.

Drover was spinning in circles and acting awfully strange. "Oh, Hank, I just can't go on, I never know what to say . . ."

"You're not supposed to *say* anything, son, just bark until we can check 'em out and give 'em clearance."

"But Hank, can you see who it is?"

I squinted and tried to focus on the pickup. About all I could come up with was that it was green. "No, who is it?"

"It's . . . Beulah."

My goodness, just the mention of her name made me weak and trembly in the legs, had to sit down and rest a minute.

"And Hank, there's somebody with her. It's . . ."

"Don't tell me, let me guess. Spotted bird dog, long skinny tail, kind of a goofy expression on his face?"

"Well . . . maybe so."

"It's Plato. She's been sweet on him for a long time and I've been waiting for a chance to clean house on him."

"What are we gonna do?"

"Stay behind me and stand by for further orders. We could get ourselves into a little skirmish here." I marched out into the lead and headed toward the pickup.

"Hank?"

"Later, son, I got violence on my mind."

"But Hank . . ."

I was too deep in concentration to be bothered with his yap. I marched up to the pickup and displayed my hardware. (In the security business, that's our way of saying that I showed him my teeth—teeth being the hardware, don't you see.)

I displayed my hardware. "So, fate brings us together at last, Plato. I thought you had better sense . . ."

"Hank."

"I thought you had better sense than to walk into my territory, Plato, but it's pretty obvious that I over-estimated your intelligence."

"Hank?"

"Shut up, Drover. But seeing as how you were foolish enough to come on my ranch, I'm calling you out. Come on, let's have a little violence and bloodshed."

Well, that must have throwed a terrible scare into him. I mean, he didn't move a muscle or make a sound, not even a squeak. "What's the matter, Plato, you lose your voice all of a sudden? It's kind of embarrassing to get exposed

34

in front of your girlfriend, ain't it?''

"Hank?''

I turned to the little noise-maker. "What?''

"You got the wrong pickup, Hank.''

"HUH?''

"They're down at the corral.''

I moved closer, sniffed the tires, checked out the sign, gave it a thorough going over. "This is the wrong pickup, Drover, and since you're in charge of eyes now, I'll have to hold you responsible. I'm afraid this will go on your record.''

"But Hank . . .''

"Drover, there's only two kinds of pickups in this world: right ones and wrong ones. This is a wrong one. Study it carefully and memorize the signs. Next time, I'll expect better information.''

"But Hank . . .''

"You think you can find the right pickup now?''

"I guess so.''

"All right, let's move out. You can go first, take the scout position, but don't forget who's running the show.''

"Okay, Hank, just follow me.''

And with that, we marched down to the cor-

ral to attend the funeral of a certain spotted
bird dog.

CHAPTER

4

SURPRISED, OR YOU MIGHT EVEN SAY SHOCKED

We went ripping down to the corral, Drover in the lead and me coming along behind. I wasn't used to taking second place, and when we got close enough so's I could kind of make out the shape of the pickup, I moved up to my proper place.

"What about Plato? Is he trembling yet?"

Drover slowed to a walk. "No, he's not, Hank. As a matter of fact . . . are you sure Plato's a bird dog?"

"Sure I'm sure."

"He's got pointed ears."

"When I get done with him, he's liable not to have any ears."

"And big teeth."

"Big, but not big enough, Drover. It's common knowledge that bird dog teeth are dull."

"They sure look sharp."

"Looks are deceiving, son. In this business you learn to trust your instincts."

I reached the pickup, and right away I caught Beulah's scent. A train-load of flowers couldn't have smelled sweeter. There was just something about that woman . . . it's hard to explain.

You'd think a guy like me—hardboiled, tested in combat, just a whisker away from being a dangerous weapon—you'd think a guy like me wouldn't respond to the softer things in this life. But the scent of Beulah did peculiar things to me.

"Morning, ma'am, and welcome to the ranch. It's always a pleasure . . ." I stopped and stared at her. It appeared to me that she'd put on a lot of weight, and her coat looked rough as a cob. "What's come over you, Beulah? You've changed, you don't have a healthy look about you."

I mean, her hair looked terrible, as coarse as straw . . .

It *was* straw. I was talking to a bale of hay on the back end of the pickup bed, must have followed the wrong scent, I mean alfalfa hay smells a lot like . . . never mind.

I kind of meandered toward the front. That eye problem was causing me entirely too much grief, and it was pretty clear that I couldn't depend on Drover to steer me in the right direction.

Technically speaking, Drover was second in command on the place. Another way of putting it is that he was *last* in command.

Drover was hopping up and down and spinning in circles. "Hi Beulah, gosh it's good to have you here on the ranch!"

"Well, thank you Drover. It's good to see you boys again."

I put a shoulder into Drover and nudged him away. "'Scuse me, son, I'll handle the women if you don't mind." I looked up into her face and my old heart began to pound. Mercy! Those big brown eyes, that silky hair, those nice ears, that fine pointed nose. "Beulah, before you got here, the day was only beautiful. Now that you're here, it's almost unbearable."

"Well, isn't that nice," she smiled. "Thank you, Hank."

"On behalf of the security division, it's my pleasure to welcome you to the ranch. If there's anything we can do to make your stay more comfortable, more interesting, more exciting, or more of anything else your heart desires . . ."

"Hank, what on earth happened to your nose?"

"Oh, just a few routine battle scars, ma'am. We had a little tussle with a silver monster bird this morning, nothing to get alarmed about. Now, if you'd like to take a little walk down to the creek . . ."

"And your eyes . . are they crossed?"

Drover hopped back into the conversation. "They sure are, but look at mine, Beulah!"

I gave him an elbow. "It's a temporary affliction, Beulah. Now . . ." I heard a growl, didn't sound like Beulah. "Was that you?"

"No Hank, it was my . . . my companion."

"Was, huh? Well, speaking of your companion, I mean since you brought the subject up, let me say this. Number one, he ain't exactly welcome on this ranch. Number two, if he can lie still and keep his yap shut, I'll try to ignore him. But, number three, if he tries that growl business again, I'm liable to feed it to him for lunch."

Would you believe that he growled again? How dumb can a bird dog be? Well, I couldn't let it slide, even though I had better things to do than to clean Plato's plow.

40

"And number four, you might tell your friend to step over here and we'll get his whipping out of the way."

All at once Drover was there beside me. "Hank, be careful. I don't think you . . ."

"I'll handle it, son. You stand by to clean up the bird dog blood."

Plato pushed Beulah aside and leaned over the edge of the pickup. That kind of surprised me. I didn't think he'd take it that far. Anyway, he leaned out and growled again.

Turned out that Drover was right. Plato *did* have sharp teeth and he *did* have pointed ears. He'd changed since I'd seen him last.

Drover was hopping up and down, and he whispered in my ear. "Hank, I don't think that's Plato."

"Huh?"

"Is Plato a . . . doberman pincher?"

"*A doberman pincher!*" I glanced up at Plato. It was all clear now. I'd made an error. I looked over at Beulah. She seemed a little uneasy. "Who is this imposter?"

"His name is Rufus, and he just moved to our ranch, and be careful, Hank, because he's very mean."

"What happened to Plato?"

"He's back at the ranch. He's afraid to come

out of the post pile because Rufus . . ."

Rufus took over from there, had kind of a nasty deep voice. "Because I whip him on sight. It's my ranch now, and I don't like bird dogs. And I don't like cowdogs with scabby noses and crossed eyes. You got anything to say about that?"

I gave it some thought. Those teeth were awful big and awful sharp. "I figger there's room in this world for differences of opinion. It just happens that I don't care a whole lot for doberman pinchers, so I guess we're about even."

"I always heard that cowdogs had a yellow streak."

I bristled at that, and it must have worried Beulah. "Hank, don't pay any attention to him. He's just a bully. Don't let him get you into a fight. That's what he wants."

She had a point there. "All right, Beulah, for you I'll let it go. Come on, Drover, we've got work to do."

Drover took off like a little rocket, heading for the feed barn. I walked away at a dignified pace. I'd gone maybe twenty steps when I heard Rufus snarl.

"You got a big mouth, Beulah. When I want your opinion, I'll ask for it."

"My opinion is that you're a brute, and I wish you'd never come to the ranch."

"Well, you better get used to it, honey, because I'm the main man in your life now. Here, gimme a little kiss, just to let me know that you really care."

I stopped.

"Keep your paws off me, you you you animal!"

"Come on, honey, just a little one." Bam! She slapped him. "You shouldn't have done that, Beulah, you just shouldn't have done that."

I turned around. Rufus bristled up and started toward her, showing all of his teeth. "Come here, woman."

"Don't you touch me!"

I headed for the pickup. "I just changed my mind, Rufus. I don't think I like your attitude, so why don't you climb down here and I'll give you a kiss you won't forget."

He stopped and stared at me. And then he laughed. "You don't know what you're asking for, cowdog."

"Just a fair chance to take you apart."

He jumped to the ground and faced me.

"When you go against a doberman, there ain't no fair chance. Just bad, worse, and disastrous."

"That's the kind of odds I like, Rufus. Come on."

"Hank, don't do it!" Beulah called. "Run away, don't try to be a hero."

I took a deep breath and looked at my lady. "It ain't a matter of trying Beulah. To some of us it just comes natural."

I faced the enemy. I was seeing double, which wasn't so good since it was hard to judge which one to fight. I picked the one on the left, sucked in my gut, and made a dive for him.

It was the wrong one. I took a ferocious bite out of the blue sky, and while I was in the air, Rufus got me, and I can't finish the story.

I'm sorry, I hate to leave things hanging but

I just can't tell the rest of it. Maybe Drover will write his memoirs one of these days and you can find out what happened.

So go on to chapter 5 but don't expect to find out about the fight.

CHAPTER

5

TOP SECRET MATERIAL

I changed my mind. Might as well go on and tell the awful truth.

I got whupped. There it is, right out in the open, and that's about the awfulest truth I can imagine.

In this big land of ours, there's a certain number of dogs that get whupped every day. But for cowdogs and heads of ranch security, it ain't a common occurrence. In fact, to some of us getting whupped is not only unpleasant, it's unthinkable.

I mean, you spend your life learning the security business. You learn tactics and strategy. You learn to use your eyes and nose and ears. You learn to cut for sign. You learn the difference between good and evil and you devote your life to protecting the good.

But fellers, it's hard to protect the good and combat evil when any old jake-legged mutt can come onto the ranch and give you a whupping. It sort of undermines your credibility.

Maybe I shouldn't pass along any classified information about the fight. I mean, I'm telling this story and I can tell it any way I choose, and I just might not choose to advertise the gloomy facts. What's to stop me from changing things around and saying that I whupped Rufus and ran him off the place, with his tail between his legs?

Well, in the first place it's fairly common knowledge that doberman pinchers don't have tails because they've been chopped off. Don't ask me why, that ain't my department, all I can say is that some dogs get their tails chopped off, and when that happens it's not possible for them to get run off a ranch with their tail between their legs because they don't have a tail, don't you see.

In the second place, if I changed the story around it would be a big nasty LIE, and furthermore I get the feeling that I'm just rambling on to avoid telling about the fight which is still a very raw spot in my memory.

All right, it's time to get serious. I'd advise you to sit down, take a deep breath, and get a good hold on your chair, because what follows is liable to be the most electrifying, terrifying, scarifying, mortifying, disturbifying and shockifying stuff you ever read.

One last word of warning before we go on. I'd suggest you lock the doors and winders and draw the blinds, and don't let the kids read this. I don't want the children to know that I got whupped.

After you've read this chapter, please cut it out of the book and burn it. It's easy to do with a pair of scissors or a knife, just . . . oh well, I guess you can figger that part out.

All right, enough said, here we go. Get hold of something stout and hang on.

W A R N I N G ! ! !

The following information is highly classified and may prove dangerous to certain individuals with high blood pressure, low blood sugar, or poor bladder control. It should be taken in small amounts and followed with periods of sleep. If unusual symptoms occur, please consult a physician immediately. You needn't consult a lawyer because dogs can't be sued.

Me and Rufus were squared off—by the way, are you sure the kids are gone and the doors are locked? Check again, just to be sure—me and Rufus squared off and faced each other.

You've seen doberman pinchers up close and you know how ugly they are—sharp-pointed ears and big teeth and them nasty little eyes, remind you of something out of a nightmare. Well, that's what I was looking at.

Some people claim that a cowdog never knows fear. I've got to dispute that. There for a second, I felt a little stab of fear, yes I did, because I wasn't facing just one doberman pincher, I was facing two. Double vision.

Up in the pickup, Beulah was saying, "No, Hank, don't do it, run for your life, he'll tear you apart, he'll kill you!"

Rufus glared at me and grinned. "You ready for this, cowdog?"

I swallered. "Ready as I'll ever be."

"You sure you want to get mauled in front of Beulah? We could go down in the bushes and do it in private."

"Suit yourself, Rufus."

He shrugged. "Well, you had your chance." He turned to Beulah. "Pay attention, woman, this is what happens to dogs that cross Rufus." Back to me. "Well, shall we dance?"

I sprang into action, made a dive for the image on the left, and as you already know, it was the wrong one. I got nothing but air, otherwise I might have . . . oh well.

Rufus caught me on the fly, when I was in mid-air, and put a deadly clamp on my neck. I tried to whirl around and get one of his ears but it was already too late. Once you get in the grip of a doberman pincher, you don't break out real easy.

That's where the name of the breed comes from, don't you see. They definitely pinch when they bite, so there you are, a little background material.

Well, once he had me in that deadly grip he pressed his advantage, which is just the sort of cheap trick you can expect from a dog that's bred and raised to be a professional bully. He throwed me to the ground. I leaped high in the air and we went around and around. But I still couldn't get out of his jaws.

Up in the pickup, Beulah was almost hysterical. "Rufus, stop it, oh please stop before someone gets hurt! Drover, do something!"

Drover had found himself a nice quiet spot inside the feed barn, but when she called he poked his head out and yipped a few times. I think you could say that Rufus wasn't worried.

Well, we snarled and growled and snapped and tore up a large area of ground, but I still couldn't get out of the pinchers. Then Rufus put me on the ground again. I was completely

wore out from the struggle. I didn't have anything left. Also, I was beginning to think the
unthinkable, that I'd been whupped on my
own ranch, in front of my assistant and the
lady of my dreams.

Rufus had them little eyes right down in my
face. Ever notice a doberman's eyes? They got
no pity in them, no feeling, and up close they
can give you the chills.

"Say calfrope."

"Rain on you."

"Say that Beulah's an ugly hag."

"Never."

"Say that you're yella."

"No."

Beulah jumped out of the pickup. "Leave
him alone, you horrible villain! Let him go!"

He turned his head and showed her some
fangs. That gave me just enough time to wiggle
out and get to my feet. We faced each other
again.

"Hank, run for your life!" Beulah cried.
"Don't be proud, run!"

"Cowdogs don't run, Beulah. We fight to
the death."

Rufus took a step toward me. "That's the
spirit. I hate to kill a dog against his will."

He crept toward me, all bunched up in his

52

shoulders and his teeth gleaming in the sun. He had a grin on his face, which was sort of disconcerting, if you know what I mean. Made a guy think he enjoyed this stuff.

Well, I was still seeing double. Last time, I'd made a dive for the image on the left, so this time I went for the one on the right and it was wrong too. Don't know how to explain that. I mean, when you try both sides and still draw a black bean, what more can you do?

I dove at him and missed. He made a slash at my throat but got me by the scruff of the neck instead. I twisted around and managed to get one of his ears. I didn't tear it off but I put a wrinkle in it.

Drover came tearing out of the feed barn, slipped between two boards in the fence, and started running in circles around us, yipping as loud as he could.

"Get him, Drover!" I yelled. "This is the fight you've been saving up for, son!"

He made a dive at Rufus and nipped him on the rump. Rufus whirled around and showed him a mouthful of teeth, which just about caused the little mutt to turn inside-out. He screeched and headed for the feed barn.

I piled into Rufus and thought I was getting the upper hand when he put a judo move on me, throwed me to the ground and landed on top of me.

I knew I was finished. I could hear Beulah crying.

Rufus got me by the throat, closed his jaws, and started digging in.

Well, as you might have guessed by now, he didn't kill me. All at once, Slim and High Loper and Billy (he lived on a ranch down the creek and always kept a bunch of mutts around, such as Plato and Rufus, and Beulah was the only good dog he'd ever owned, if you ask me), all at once, Slim and High Loper and Billy were there, yelling and trying to pull us apart.

"Here, Roof, down boy, hyah, cut that out!"

Billy took his pet dragon by the collar and dragged him a short distance away. Loper held me back. "Billy, that's quite a dog you've got there."

"He's bad, ain't he? I figgered I needed a dog around that could take care of business. Say, I thought old Hank was a better fighter than that."

Loper looked down at me. "So did I."

I wagged my tail and whimpered. Couldn't he see that my dadgum eyes were crossed? I

mean, how can a dog fight with Eye-Crosserosis?

Loper didn't notice. "I guess he's showing his age. You don't think about these dogs getting old, but they do, same as the rest of us. Well, Hank, anything broke?"

Only my heart, but I didn't expect him to care about that.

"Well," Billy said, "guess I'd better take this beast home before he does any more damage. Y'all come see us."

"Sure will. Y'all too."

They got into the pickup and drove off. I'll

never forget the expression on Beulah's face as they pulled out. She just looked at me with big sad eyes while Roof-Roof sat on the bale of hay like a king on his throne.

When they were gone, Loper reached down and rubbed me behind the ears. "Well, Hank, I guess you're not the top dog in the neighborhood any more. Kinda hurts, don't it?"

Loper and Slim went back to work and left me there alone. It kinda hurt, yes it did.

(FINAL NOTE: Don't forget to destroy this chapter. And don't let the kids find out what happened.)

6

DROVER TURNS ON THE DEAREST FRIEND HE HAS IN THIS WORLD

Everyone left and I limped and dragged myself toward the gas tanks, figgered I needed a long spell of rest because I was so sore and beat up from the fight.

I'd gone maybe twenty-five steps when it occurred to me that I couldn't *see* the gas tanks, didn't know exactly which way to go, and was too wore out to get there anyway.

I mean, that doberman had given me a terrible beating. My throat hurt, my neck hurt, my ears had been chewed up. I was limping on one front leg and packing one of the back ones. When you were built to be a four-legged creature, it's hard to motivate on two.

I found the corral fence and followed it

around to the gate in front of the saddle shed. That was as far as I could go. I flopped down and waited for help to arrive. I knew Drover would be along directly and he could lead me down to the gas tanks and help me into bed.

I waited and waited. Drover didn't show up. Couldn't understand that. You'd think the little guy would come around just as soon as he was sure the coast was clear. I mean, when the Head of Ranch Security is out of commission, that's cause for concern, right?

About half an hour later, I heard something off to the south. With considerable effort, I lifted my head and looked in that direction. Couldn't see anything but a blur, but my ears are pretty keen and I got a good reading on the sound.

It was kind of a click-click-click, made by a four-legged animal with a short stride. The click part came from little claws hitting the hard ground.

It was Drover, I knew it was. "Drover, I'm over here!"

I cocked my head and listened. Whoever it was didn't answer. He broke into a run and took off to the east, and in a minute the sound was gone.

That was strange. Why would Drover take

off like that? Surely he knew I'd been beat up and needed some help.

Well, I thought about it and came up with an answer. Drover was out looking for me and with his poor vision and dead nose, he just hadn't located me yet. He'd find me after a bit.

But why had he run when he heard me call? That was a little harder to fit into the picture, but you know, when a guy wants the picture to come out right, he'll find ways of making it. Facts don't squeal when you stuff 'em where you want 'em to go.

I told myself that Drover was still shook up over the big fight and hadn't got his nerves under control yet. My voice had scared him. He'd come around after a while.

Well, the hours dragged on and still no Drover. The afternoon sun got blistering hot and the wind blew sand in my eyes. Along toward the end of the day, I was feeling mighty weak and thirsty and decided I'd better give up waiting for Drover. I mean, it might take him another half-day to find me.

So I pushed myself up on all two legs (I was packing the other two, remember) and limped over in front of the saddle shed door, where the cowboys were sure to find me when they shut down for the night. It couldn't have been more than ten-twelve steps, but it took all my energy just to get there.

I flopped down, curled up in a ball, and waited. Sure 'nuff, at sundown Slim and Loper came along and put their saddle-horses up for the night.

I was in perfect position. They couldn't put their saddles up without seeing me there, and I felt sure that once they saw my wretched condition, they'd give me some well-deserved sympathy and maybe carry me down to the gas tanks.

Slim pulled off his saddle and came up to the door. His eyes were red from the dirt and the wind, and he looked tired. "Move, Hank, I got to get in." I lifted my head and whapped my tail and whined, figgered that would give him a hint that I was stove up. "Well, suit yourself."

He opened the door, stepped over me, and went inside, dragging his saddle. I took a lick from all four cinches and both stirrups, and I mean that last one hurt.

Then Loper came. He looked down at me and muttered something under his breath, then he tried to walk over me and stepped on my tail and so naturally I yelped.

What's so bad about that? I mean, my tail's

alive and when you step on it it hurts, and
when it hurts I yelp. Seems reasonable to me.

But Loper stumbled and I guess he got sore
about it. "Hank, for crying out loud, do you
have to park yourself right in the middle of
traffic?"

Slim came over to the door and looked

down at me. "He acts like he don't feel real good."

Well, at last we were getting somewhere. I whapped my tail to let 'em know that they were on the right track.

Then Loper said, "If he can't whip these dogs any more, he's gonna have to learn to stay out of fights." They stepped over me and closed up the shed. "If you can't handle Billy's dog, then next time he comes around you better go to the house, you hear? When your body fails, you have to use your brain, if you've got one."

That's the kind of sympathy you get around this ranch. All they expect is a twenty-four-hour day, a perfect record, and a pint of blood every now and then just to prove . . . oh well.

A guy can't afford to get worked up about injustice. It's worse than running rabbits.

Darkness fell and there I was, all alone, curled up in a ball of hair with the wind blowing dirt in my face. The moon came up and the coyotes started howling. If they'd known my condition, they could have ravaged the place, I mean swept down and pillaged it from one end to the other.

I could only hope they wouldn't launch an attack, because ranch security was at its most dangerous level in many years.

At last I drifted off to sleep. Don't recall what time it was when I woke up. I heard some noise out there between the saddle shed and the house. My usual response would have been to leap into action and sound the alarm, but I wasn't up to my usual response. I growled. That was about the best I could do.

"Who's out there? State your name and your business or I'll . . . who's there?"

There was a moment of silence, then I heard Drover's voice. "Hank? You okay?"

"No, I'm not okay, and what do you mean, creeping around in the night?"

"Oh, I was up and thought I ought to come check on you."

"Well you sure took your time getting here. Where the devil have you been?"

"I got busy with some things, Hank, and just never got around."

"Get over here, so I won't have to yell. My throat hurts."

He came closer but stopped about ten feet away. He seemed kind of uneasy about something. "This better?"

"Is there some reason why you can't come over here where I am? I ain't got scabies."

"I know that, but I . . . Hank, I don't want

to see you this way. I guess that's why I didn't come around sooner."

"What do you mean by that? I'm the same Hank only a little beat up."

"That's what I mean. Beat up." He looked down at his feet and kind of shuffled around. "I've seen you fight monsters and coyotes and coons, and you always won. I guess I thought . you see what I mean?"

"Yeah, it's coming clear. A guy loses one fight and all his so-called friends think he's over the hill. Is that what you're saying?"

"It makes a guy wonder. I don't know what to think."

"Why you little pipsqueak! Just for that, I'm gonna . . ." I pushed myself up and started after him. Went two steps and fell down, just didn't have the energy to thrash him.

"That's what I mean, Hank. You ought to give me a licking for saying all this stuff . . . but you can't. I can do anything I want to do . . . but I don't know what I want to do. I'm all confused."

"You're definitely confused."

"But see, I know that if I wanted to stick my tongue out at you—like this—I could do it."

He did it, stuck his tongue out at me. "Watch it, Drover, you're breeding a scab on

the end of your nose.''

"And I got a suspicion that if I wanted to parade in front of you—like this—I could do it too.''

And that's just what the runt did, paraded in front of me *and* stuck out his tongue. I took a snap at him, but he was out of my range.

"Drover, you're courting disaster.''

"And Hank, I have an idea that I could even throw some dirt on you and get by with it.''

"I wouldn't try that, son.''

"I know you wouldn't, and I wouldn't either . . . only I just want to. Like this.'' He scratched the ground with his paw and threw dirt on me.

I couldn't believe he did that. On a better day, I would have torn him apart, I mean ripped him up one side and down the other. But I had to lie there and take it. I managed to growl, but that was my best lick.

"Okay, Drover, you did it. You happy now?"

"No, I feel awful, I hate myself, I just don't know what to think any more . . . only I bet I could do it again." And he did it again, threw dirt on me, stuck out his tongue, and went prancing back and forth.

Then he started crying. "Oh Hank, why did you have to get whipped? I was happy the way things were, but now I just feel like a louse! Tell me what to do."

I shook the dirt off. "All right, I'll tell you what to do. First thing, say you're sorry. Second thing, go up to the gas tank and say 'I will be more respectful to the Head of Ranch Security' a thousand times. And then go out on patrol and take care of the ranch."

"All of that?"

"Yes sir, every bit of it."

He rolled his eyes and looked up at the stars. "But Hank, I don't want to . . . and I don't have to . . . because you can't make me."

I stared at him. "Then why did you ask?"

"I don't know. I better go, Hank, before I make you mad."

"You're a little late for that, son."

He started backing away. "I'm sorry, Hank, I really am. I just wanted to find out . . ."

He took off and that was the last I saw of the sawed-off, stub-tailed, ungrateful little wretch. But all through the night I heard him. You think he was out on patrol? Taking care of the ranch? Keeping an eye on the chickenhouse? Checking for coons?

No sir, he was out there playing peekaboo with Pete the Barncat.

CHAPTER

7

TRICKED, LED ASTRAY, AND ABANDONED TO A TERRIBLE FATE

I had thought that maybe I would be better come morning, but I was worse. Not only did I ache and throb from nose to tail, but I was getting weak from hunger and thirst.

And as if that wasn't enough, along about ten o'clock in the morning the ants and flies started moving in on me.

It started with a couple of big green flies buzzing around my ears. Well, you know me. I don't allow that, never have. I sat up and took defensive action. I snapped and growled and sent one of them to fly heaven, which was very satisfying but not so good in the taste department. Never did care for the taste of green flies.

The other one kept it up. Then there were two and four and ten and twenty, and I was wore out and couldn't keep them away. Finally I laid my head down and gave up.

They crawled over my nose, buzzed in my ears, walked around my eyes, and bit me on the rump, which really hacked me off but I didn't have the energy to fight back.

Then came the ants, those little black villains that march in single file and contribute absolutely nothing to this world, except they sting innocent victims and drive you nuts. Why were they put on this earth? You got me.

They came in rows and columns, marching up to me in unending lines. I don't know what they expected to find or why they singled me out, but by ten-thirty I had become a major population center for ants.

They crawled up my tail and just by George moved in. They were in my hair, on my face, inside my ears and nose and mouth, and when they found something they didn't approve of, they just stung it.

Hateful little things.

I tried to fight them off for a while, but there

was no end to them, they just kept coming. I was too tired and weak and hungry to fight any more, so I gave up. Heck, if they wanted to eat me alive, that was okay with me, long as I didn't have to put out any effort.

I guess it was around noon when Slim and Loper came around. I must have looked pretty ragged by then because I got their attention.

Loper bent down and started picking ants off my face. "Say, this dog's not doing any good. What's wrong, Hank?"

I lifted my head and gave him a wooden stare. What was wrong? I'd been defeated in battle, wounded, abandoned, mocked, and abused. I was thirsty, half-starved, wind-blown, sunburned, and tormented by ants and flies. My spirit was smashed, my heart was broken, and I didn't give a rip whether I lived or died.

Other than that, it was a pretty nice day.

Slim bent down too. I heard his knees pop. "Maybe we better get him some food, reckon? You want some grub, Hankie?"

Slim stayed at the saddle shed and Loper went up to the house. He came back with a bowl of milk and eggs. I would have preferred scrambled eggs. It takes too much energy to eat them raw. I mean, you got to chase down the slimy part and get a handle on it before you can eat it.

But in this life you don't always get your eggs scrambled.

I got to admit that the boys were pretty nice to me this time. I mean, it came about twenty-four hours too late, but at least they made an effort. They set the bowl down in front of my nose and went on to lunch.

I took a few bites and decided maybe it was worth the trouble of eating, when all at once guess who came along, rubbing up against the fence, purring like a little chain saw, and holding his tail high in the air. You got it. Pete.

I stopped eating and gave him a withering glare.

"Umm, hi Hankie, time to eat?"

"Scram, cat. I got no time for your foolishness."

"Where'd you get all the flies?"

"I got lonesome."

He grinned and sharpened his claws on a fencepost. "What would you take for some milk and eggs, Hankie? I just *love* milk and eggs."

"I'd take one of your legs and about six inches off that tail. Beat it."

He looked at his claws and rubbed against the post and moved toward the bowl in his typical dumb-cat manner, purring and switching the tip of his tail.

I don't know what it is about that tail-switching, but it just don't sit right with me. There's something about it that gets me stirred up. I glared at him and growled.

He walked up to the edge of the bowl, flicked his paw into the milk, and licked it. "Ummm! That's mighty tasty, Hankie. How come they're giving you milk and eggs today? That's pretty plush treatment for a dog . . ." He turned and curled the end of his tail around my nose. ". . . that got whipped."

I snapped at him, missed amputating his tail by just a matter of inches. "I'll plush *your* treatment if you don't get that tail out of my face."

He grinned. "How come your eyes are crossed, Hankie?"

"It's the latest style."

"It must be hard to be cocky when you're cross-eyed, hmm?"

"I'll manage. Stick that tail over here one more time and I'll show you."

He did, I snapped, I missed, he grinned. "Strike two, Hankie. Your aim's not what it used to be. That's sure too bad because," he took a big stretch and dug his claws into the dirt, "because I just might try to steal your milk."

"You touch my milk and you're a dead cat."

"Bet you can't stop me."

I pushed myself up to a sitting position—with considerable effort, I might add—and prepared for combat. "You just try it."

He reached out his paw and touched the surface of the milk, ever so lightly. "I touched it."

He touched off a by George explosion, is what he touched. I didn't think I had enough energy to romp a cat, but come to find out I did. I made a slash at him and missed. He walked away, flicking his tail and grinning at me over his shoulder.

"Strike three, Hankie. Bet you can't catch me."

I lunged at him and got him. Well, I got some hairs off the end of his tail, actually, but that was enough to make me want some more. I made another pounce at him.

He squirmed out of my grip and went padding across the pasture toward the creek. Ordinarily he would have made a dash for the nearest tree but this time he didn't.

Well, this gave me a valuable piece of

G.L. Holmes

information and I began to formulate an overall strategy and plan of battle, which is one of the normal procedures we use in the security business.

One of the major advantages a cowdog has over a cat is that your ordinary run-of-the-mill cat is flighty and impulsive, while your cowdog applies mental discipline to every problem. I think most experts would back me up on this.

I mean, let's face it: it's a well-known fact that cats act on whim and impulse and lack the mental whatever-it-is to think in terms of a long range strategy. Some authorities would say they're fairly stupid animals, which is what I would say.

Pete's behavior offered a classic example of this. Instead of staying close to the big trees around the corral, he headed down toward the creek, where the trees tended to be small and scrubby: creek willows and tamaracks instead of elms and cottonwoods.

In other words, Pete had made a crucial mistake which any dog trained in security work would never make: he had become cocky and careless and had allowed himself to be lured away from his best defensive position.

Once I had my basic strategy in mind, I followed the cat out into the pasture and down into the creek willows, keeping him in sight and waiting for my big opportunity. We call this "lulling the enemy." As Uncle Beanie used to say, "Lull 'em to sleep and then wake 'em up in the rudest possible manner."

I must have stalked him for a mile or more, far enough from the house so that it was unfamiliar territory. I figured that was far enough. The time had come. The bell was tolling for whom the bell was tolling for.

He was maybe five feet in front of me. I gathered all my strength, threw it into one mighty lunge, and didn't lunge because my knees went out on me.

All at once I was so weak I couldn't stand up. I laid down and tried to catch my breath. Felt a little fuzzy in the head.

Pete was grinning, another indication that he didn't understand the seriousness of his situation. "Nice day for a walk, isn't it Hankie?"

"Give me a minute to catch my breath and I'll show you how nice a day it is." Sure was feeling weak.

Pete yawned and stretched. "Tell me something, Hankie. With your eyes crossed, how will you find your way back home?"

"HUH?"

"I need to get back and finish your milk and eggs. You followed me out here but you won't be following me back. It might be hard to find the ranch."

Hadn't thought of it exactly in those terms. "Wait a minute, cat. *You* walked into *my* trap, so don't be trying to . . ."

"See you around, Hankie." He walked away, switching his tail and purring. He glanced back at me and winked. "If you need anything, just give me a call."

"Don't think you can bluff me, cat. Hey, come back here! Pete? Hey listen, I was only

. . . let's talk this thing over . . .''

How the devil had I got myself in this mess?

As the afternoon wore on, I began to suspect that I was in a whole gob of trouble.

8

THE CHOPPED CHICKEN LIVER MYSTERY

There's no pleasant way of describing my situation. I was in deep trouble, and with night coming on, it was getting deeper and deeper. Let's face it: the ranch was a dangerous place even in broad daylight, but at night, when the forces of darkness came out, it was no place for the faint-hearted.

When the sun slipped over the horizon, I felt the dampness rising from the ground and a shiver of dread passed through my battered carcass. Up the creek a ways, I heard the mournful hoot of an owl, and overhead the swish of a bullbat's wings.

And little footsteps out there in the dark—mice, packrats, lizards, frogs, snakes, a guy didn't know what kind of creature might be creeping around out there, only I'll have to admit that snakes don't have feet so they don't make footsteps, but that's pretty creepy in itself, an animal that slithers and doesn't have the common decency to make a sound.

Me and snakes never did get along, just don't like 'em at all, the way they sneak and slither and slide and glide through the grass, and if I don't quit talking about snakes I'm going to get myself worked into a scare. No more about snakes.

There were no snakes out there slithering through the grass so that was one less thing I had to worry about, although I kept hearing this slithering sound out there in the grass. Sounded a lot like snakes, but I knew in my heart that it was big worms. I ain't scared of worms, even big ones.

I was feeling mighty small and helpless, curled up there in a ball with one ear perked up to monitor the sounds of the night, when all at once I heard a different kind of noise.

Heavy footsteps, the crackle of brush, the rumble of voices, and then . . . singing? Impossible. Nobody but a bunch of drunken coyotes would be singing at that hour of the night. I held my breath and listened.

Me just a worthless coyote, me howling at
the moon.
Me like to sing and holler, me crazy as a
loon.
Me not want job or duties, no church or
Sunday school,
Me just a worthless coyote and me ain't
nobody's fool.

Well, I certainly recognized that song, and I had a suspicion that I knew the guys who were singing it. Rip and Snort, the two coyote brothers.

I'd had some good times with those boys, back during my outlaw days, but I'd last seen them on the field of battle when I had single-handedly turned back an invasion of the entire coyote nation and saved the chickenhouse from a massacre.

I had some pretty fierce hand-to-hand combat with Rip and Snort, and I didn't figger they'd be real friendly if they caught me out there all by myself, half-blind and helpless.

I held my breath, hoping they would pass by. They came closer and closer. They were so busy singing and carrying on, I thought they'd miss me.

But all at once the singing stopped. Silence. I could hear my heart thumping. A twig snapped close by. I heard them whispering.

I turned my head around and looked into the sharp-nosed, yellow-eyed face of a coyote. "Well, if it isn't . . . I'll be derned . . . how in the world are you doing, Snort, by George it's great to see you boys again."

They stared at me.

"Been a long time, hasn't it?"

I could tell they were thinking.

"How's the family? How's old Scraunch getting along, just as ornery as ever, I bet."

They were still thinking. Rip and Snort were never what you'd call rapid thinkers.

"How come Hunk out here alone?"

"Alone? Well, that's . . . pretty obvious, isn't it? I mean . . . maybe it's not so obvious, huh?"

"Not so obvious."

I had a feeling that what I said here would be crucial to my survival. That's a lot of pressure, especially when you're in poor health.

"Well uh . . . fellers, I could tell you what I'm doing out here but you wouldn't believe it, I mean it's just the wildest craziest thing you ever heard in your life. You wouldn't believe it, would you?"

"Hear first, then decide."

"It'll take special powers of belief, and unless you guys think you can handle it, I'd rather not get into it."

They sat down. "Tell story," said Rip.

I glanced over both shoulders and lowered my voice. "Listen, I wouldn't be out here if this wasn't pretty derned special. I came alone because I didn't want anybody else to know about it. And if you should happen to pry this out of me, you've got to promise me three things."

They traded glances. "What promises?"

"First off, you've got to promise never to tell anyone about it. If news of this ever got out . . . well, it could be very serious. You promise never to tell?"

"We promise."

"All right, second thing is, you've got to follow the directions exactly and to the letter. One little mistake could cause a catastrophe."

Rip narrowed his eyes. "What means, catastrophe?"

"It means boom! Fire, explosion, black smoke in the sky, thunder and lightning, famine and drought, dead birds falling out of trees, the whole nine yards. You sure you want to know?"

They went into a huddle and talked it over. Then Snort said, "We take the chance."

"All right, now we're down to the last promise. You've got to promise to believe everything I tell you, no matter how crazy it sounds."

Snort shook his head. "Not work. Hear first, then decide. Snort not believe every crazy stuff that come along."

I was real sorry to hear that because the stuff

84

I had in mind was pretty crazy. The brothers were getting restless. Snort got to his feet and stuck his sharp nose in my face.

"Better you tell or we have big fight, oh boy."

"All right, all right, relax. Look, Snort, you agreed to Promise Number Two, right? Promised to follow all the directions, right?"

"Right, that one okay."

"One of the directions is that you have to believe the story."

Snort and Rip looked at each other, and Snort said, "Uh."

"But I'll be reasonable about it. Since you've already agreed to believe the story, I'll drop the third promise. Would that make you feel better?"

Snort sat down and scratched his ear for a minute. "Very complicated, not quite understand."

"Yeah, but a promise is a promise. That's simple enough. What do you say, shall we scratch Number Three?"

Snort stared at me. "Scratch ear, got fleas."

"I mean, shall we drop Promise Number Three? That's the best I can do."

"We make talk." They went into a huddle and talked it over in whispers. Then Snort said, "Okay, we make deal. Drop Promise Three, keep One and Two."

"When it comes to driving a bargain, you guys are tough."

"We very tough, fighting a lot and singing coyote song."

"Well, are you ready for this?"

Their heads bobbed up and down. "We ready."

"Then here goes. See that moon up there? Would you believe it's made of chopped chicken liver?" They shook their heads. "But you've already promised to believe it." They bobbed their heads up and down.

"Now, would you believe the moon can come down from the sky and land right here on the ground? And would you believe you can eat that chopped chicken liver until you bust?" They shook their heads. "But you already promised you'd believe it." They bobbed their heads up and down.

"And would you believe that if you two guys stuck your heads into opposite ends of a hollow log and counted to fifty thousand by ones, *it would make the moon come down?*"

Rip shook his head, but Snort raised his paw. "Ha! We already promise believe!" He looked at me and grinned. "Brother not catch on yet." And Rip nodded his head.

"Well, there you are, guys, now you know the whole story. But I hope you don't think I'm going to let you have the first shot at the chicken liver."

"Heh, Hunk not catch on either. Rip and Snort get whole moon, eat sick, throw up and eat some more, oh boy. Hunk good dog, sing pretty good, but not smart like coyote."

"Hey listen . . ." With great effort, I pushed myself up, and with very little effort, Snort pushed me back down.

"Stay here. Maybe we bring one liver. Now we find hollow log, count to many thousand. So long, Hunk."

"But what about . . . hey, wait . . ."

They plunged into the darkness, yipping and howling and laughing their heads off. I didn't waste a minute. I dragged myself down to the creek, slipped into a deep pool, and swam across to the other side.

I didn't want to be around come morning.

9

INVITED FOR
BREAKFAST

As you might have already figgered out by now, I went into the creek for two reasons: because it's easier to swim than to walk when you're stove up, and because you don't leave a scent in the water. I didn't want those two brothers following my scent.

I swam as far as I could, until the creek got too shallow, and then I climbed out and started walking. The swim must have done me some good because my aches and pains felt better when I got out. But I still had that Eye-Crosserosis problem, and I had no idea where I was going.

I walked until I came to a big cottonwood tree, and that's where I stopped for the night. Didn't sleep too soundly, kept having the same bad dream about getting whupped on my own ranch by a doberman pincher. Sounds familiar, don't it?

What woke me up was the sound of voices, two of them, and I knew that Rip and Snort had tracked me down and were fixing to stomp a mudhole in Hank the Cowdog. I just wasn't ready for that.

I opened my eyes and looked around. Couldn't see anyone, not even a blurred image of anyone. But then I heard the voices again, coming from the tree above me. I'd heard those voices before. They belonged to a couple of buzzards.

"Junior, you git outa that bed and go find us some breakfast!"

"But P-Pa . . ."

"It's shameful the way you mope around in the mornings. Why, when I was your age . . ."

"But P-Pa . . ."

". . . I was up every morning at daylight, yes I was, out looking for food. Do you want to know what your trouble is, son?"

"N-n-n-not really, not really."

"The trouble with you is you're lazy and shiftless, yes sir, and you seem to think our grub's gonna come walking up and park itself at the bottom of this tree. But life isn't that way, son, I've told you and I've told you."

"P-P-Pa?"

"What!"

"I th-think something w-w-walked up and p-p-p-p-parked itself at the bottom bottom bottom of this t-t-t-t-tree, tree, cause there's something dee-dee-duh-down there."

There was a long silence, then Wallace said, "And the other trouble with you, Junior, is that you have this smart alecky streak. Nobody likes a smart aleck, son, what is that thang down there?"

"B-beats me, but it's g-g-got t-two tails and a ear."

"You mean two ears and a tail?"

"Th-that's what I su-su-su-said."

"You reckon it'll eat?"

"I bu-bet it will, 'cause I'm h-hungry."

"Follow me, son, and always remember that your elders get first dibs. I want a leg."

I glanced up and saw Wallace spread his wings and step off the branch. He flapped as hard as he could, but he must have miscalculated because he flew right into a tangle of grapevines that were hanging on a big tree nearby. He squawked and flapped and tried to get out, but he got a leg caught and ended up hanging upside-down.

"Dang the luck!" Now look what you've got
me into!"

Junior stepped off the branch, flapped his
wings, and crashed on the ground. The impact
drove his beak into the dirt and he got up
spitting.

"Junior! Get me down from here! Don't you
dare take a bite, not one bite, until I get there."

Junior ignored him. He had a crazy grin on

his face and came jumping toward me. I raised up and growled and showed him some fangs. He stopped in his tracks, and you should have seen that smile disappear. It just by George melted.

"Oh d-d-darn!"

"Junior!" the old man yelled. "There's no call for cussin'. Now you just watch your language."

Junior turned and looked up at him. "Well, you c-c-cuss all the t-time."

"Son, there's a time for cussin' and a time for not cussin', and when you get old enough to know right from wrong, we'll let you try it, but there's no call for cussin' at this particular time, git me out of this tree!"

Junior glanced at me again. I gave him another growl and he edged a few steps away. "P-pa, it's hu-hu-hu-him again, him again, that same d-d-dog."

"What?"

"And he he he ain't du-dead again."

As I said, Wallace was hanging upside-down. He stared at me and I stared at him, and for good measure I gave 'em another growl.

"Well I'll be . . . of all the dad-danged, gosh-blamed, stinking, horrifying, son-of-a-gun pig-nosed lousy luck!"

"P-P-Pa? You're c-cussin'."

"You dang right I'm cussin'! When it's time to cuss, a guy needs to do it right, and further-more, you git me out of this tree right now, you hear me, or I'll . . ."

"Y-you'll wha-wha-what, Pa?"

"I'll . . ." Just then his foot came loose and he crashed to the ground. ". . . be danged, like to of broke my neck, but you don't care, all you ever think about is yourself because the trouble with you, son, is that you've got no respect for age and wisdom, is what's wrong with you."

"I th-thought the tr-trouble with me was that . . ."

Wallace straightened his neck and came waddling over. "You got lots of troubles, is the trouble with you." He came over and glared down at me. "Shame on you!"

"Well, shame on you right back!"

That straightened him up. "Junior, did you hear that? Are you gonna just stand there and take that off a dog?"

Junior peeked around the old man. "M-most likely I w-will, Pa, most l-likely, cause he m-m-might b-b-bite."

"Well, I never . . . when I was your age . . ." The old man rubbed his beak with the end of his wing and scowled. "Say there, neighbor, aren't you the same one who give us a chicken head one time?"

"Yep."

"I don't reckon you got another one."

"Nope."

"Didn't figger you did, sure could use one though."

Just then I had a brilliant idea. "Speaking of that chicken head, seems to me you boys promised to do me a favor some time."

The old man shook his head. "I don't recall that, sure don't."

"W-w-we did, Pa, w-we sure d-d-did."

Wallace snapped his head toward Junior. "And *you* can just *hush,* you don't have to tell everything you know!" Back to me. "Maybe we did, maybe we did."

"Well, I'm here to collect."

"Eh, what exactly did you have in mind, neighbor? We've had some bad luck lately and . . ."

I explained about the Eye-Crosserosis problem and how I was lost and couldn't find my way back to the ranch. All of a sudden Wallace seemed mighty interested.

"I see what you mean, yes. A guy could starve to death out here."

"I b-b-bet Madame M-Moonshine could f-f-f-fix his uh-uh-eyes, fix his eyes."

Me and the old man turned and stared at Junior, and I said, "Who's Madame Moonshine?"

"You hush your mouth, Junior, don't you . . ."

"She's a wu-wu-wu-witch and lives in a ca-ca-cave, in a cave."

"She's a witch? And lives in a cave?"

"No, she's no such thing," Wallace butt in, "and she don't live in no cave, and Junior you leave the talking to me, and as for you," he looked at me, "we can't help you."

I got to my feet and went nose-to-nose with the old man. "Listen, you old bucket of guts, I gave you a chicken head and I'm fixing to collect a *buzzard's* head unless you take me to Madame Moonshine. Pronto."

"Well, you don't have to be so tacky about it. I just thought, see what you done, Junior?"

"I d-done right, P-Pa, cause he's our f-friend."

"Friend," Wallace muttered. "The only friend a buzzard's got is his next meal. Wouldn't hurt you to remember that."

Wallace went waddling through the willows, still grumbling to himself, and me and

Junior fell in behind him.

Up ahead, I could hear Wallace carrying on: ". . . danged kids . . . tried to tell the boy . . . stubborn, mule-headed . . . never amount to bird hockey . . ."

It was quite a procession, two waddling buzzards and one jake-legged dog. As we walked along, Junior told me about Madame Moonshine. Said she was a burrowing owl, used to live in a prairie dog town (which is where you find most burrowing owls, don't you see), only the prairie dogs ran her out of town because she had a witchy kind of power.

Sounded pretty strange to me.

We picked our way through the willows, until at last we came to a rocky ledge on the south bank of the creek. Wallace stopped and pointed to a cave.

"There it is. This is as far as we go. She's in there somewhere."

I turned to Junior. "You sure this is the right thing to do?"

"I b-b-bet she can f-fix you."

"Well, thanks again." I started up the ledge. When I went past the old man, he curled his lip at me.*

"G-G-Good luck," Junior called. "And w-w-watch out for the s-s-s-snakes!"

"HUH?"

"Rattlesnakes," said Wallace, "dozens of 'em, place is crawling with 'em. And say, if you get bit, try to make it outside the cave before you die, would you? I'd like for something to come of this friendship."

I tried to think of a brilliant reply, something slashing and witty that would really put the old bird in his place. Sometimes I can come up with brilliant replies and sometimes I can't. This time I couldn't.

I headed for the cave, feeling just a little shaky about them snakes, not to mention the witch. I'd never met a witch before.

---

*Some bird experts would probably point out here that buzzards don't have lips, so Wallace couldn't have curled his lip at me. Okay, maybe he didn't, but he did something with his beak that certainly gave that impression.

H.C.D

10

MADAME MOONSHINE

I climbed the ledge and stuck my head into the cave, sniffed, checked things out. It looked suspicious to me.

I'm not the kind of dog who enjoys holes. Some do, I guess, but not me. I got locked into a big wooden tack box when I was a kid, and since then I've tried to avoid places that are dark and closed in.

I started inside the cave, got a creepy feeling, and backed out. Figgered I'd better study on it a little more before I did anything drastic. I mean, Junior had said something about snakes, and you know where I stand on the snake issue.

How did I know that Madame Moonshine could cure Eye-Crosserosis? In fact, how did I know that Madame Moonshine even existed?

All I had to go on was the word of a couple of buzzards, and in the security business we tend to give low priority to the testimony of buzzards.

I'd just about talked myself out of going in there when I realized I had some company. I was peering inside the cave, see, and happened to glance to my left and saw a little owl—a burrowing owl, in fact, which I thought was an interesting coincidence. She was peering into the cave too.

"What's in there?" she whispered. She had big yellow eyes, and I noticed she had a way of rolling her head around without moving her body.

"I don't know, ma'am. I've been told that someone called Madame Moonshine hangs out here. I don't suppose you know anything about her, do you? They say she's a witch or something."

The lady's head twisted around and she stared at me with them big eyes. "You believe in witches?"

"Well, I don't know for sure. Never met one."

"I don't believe in them, and I've met several. But I don't believe in dogs either, so there you are."

"How come you don't believe in dogs? I mean, I'm a dog myself."

"Well, that's only your opinion. Everyone has an opinion."

I couldn't help chuckling at that. "Yeah, but I'm Head of Ranch Security, see. Maybe you didn't realize that. You might say that I run this ranch, so my opinion carries a little weight."

"Ah! So *you* run this ranch?"

"Yes ma'am, and have for several years. There's very little that goes on around here without my say-so."

"I see. Do you make the sun rise?"

"Uh . . . not exactly."

"Do you tell the trees when to shed their leaves?"

"Well . . . no."

"Did you teach the fish to swim?"

"No ma'am."

She bent down and looked at the ground. "There's an ant. Would you mind telling him to go somewhere else?"

I was feeling a little uncomfortable about this. "I guess I could try. Ant, scram, go on, get out of here!" It didn't work.

The lady gave me a puzzled look. "Now tell me again: what is it that you do?"

"I'm Head of . . . look, ants don't listen to

anybody, they just ain't smart enough."

Now get this. She spread out her wings and brought them together in front, so they pointed toward the ant, and she made a kind of whistling sound. The derned fool ant stopped in his tracks, turned around, and ran away.

The lady looked at me and grinned and blinked her eyes. "I'm sorry, what were you saying?"

"Nuthin." Then all at once it struck me. All the clues came together. I had figgered it out. "Wait a minute! I bet you're Madame Moonshine."

"Oh yes I am! And you're Hank the Rabbit."

"Huh? No, I'm Hank the Cowdog."

"Of course! Yes, I see now. Won't you come in?"

I squinted into that dark hole and gave it another sniffing. "You got any snakes in there?"

"How many did you want?"

"I don't want any, I'm scared of 'em."

"Oh rubbish, just tell them who you are. Come, follow me."

She hopped into the hole. I swallered real hard and went in behind her. It was pretty narrow and it got dark all of a sudden. I'd gone five or six feet when I started hearing a bunch of hissing and rattling and felt cold things crawling around.

It was them dadgum snakes. I couldn't turn around, I couldn't back out, so I crawled forward just as fast as I could. For a while I could hear Madame Moonshine hopping in front of me, but then all I could hear was hissing and rattling.

"Ma'am?" No answer. I began to suspect that I'd made an error in judgment. I mean, Eye-Crosserosis is pretty bad stuff, but it beats the heck out of Dead-Doggerosis.

The cave turned to the left, and up ahead I could see a big chamber with a shaft of sunlight coming down. I crawled toward it as fast as I could.

I was out of breath when I got there, and when I looked around there was no sign of Madame Moonshine. I sat down and waited. Heard a sound off to my left, turned, and saw a huge, enormous diamondback rattlesnake slipping toward me. He was flicking his tongue out and he had a wicked look in his eyes.

My first instinct was to build a new door in the roof, but then I remembered what Madame Moonshine had said. I held my ground and tried to get control of the shakes.

"I'm Hank the Cowdog," I said in my gruffest voice, "Head of Ranch Security." He kept coming. "Maybe you didn't hear me. I said I'm Hank the Cowdog, Head of Ranch Security."

That was supposed to do the trick, but it didn't. The snake built a coil at my feet and started buzzing.

I thought I was finished, fellers, but just then Madame Moonshine's head popped out of a hole in the cave wall. "Back again! Oh, you've met Timothy, and my goodness, I think he's going to bite you. Didn't you tell him who you are? Timothy, shame on you! Go away, shoo! This is the *Head of Ranch Security*."

The snake slipped away into the gloom. She came out of the hole in the wall and hopped over to the place where the sunlight hit the floor. "Now, tell me why you're here."

I told her the whole story, about how my eyes had crossed and how Rufus had whupped up on me, how Pete had suckered me out into the wilderness, the buzzards, everything.

While I told the story, she picked up a lizard bone in her claws and chewed on it, and every now and then she would give her head a nod.

"You think you can help me, Madame?"

She pitched the bone aside and wiped her mouth on her wing. "Maybe and maybe not. We'll have to test you. How many fingers am I holding up?"

I squinted at her. "Uh . . . three?"

"No! I'm holding NO fingers up. Owls HAVE no fingers. Can you read the letters on this chart?"

I squinted again. "Ma'am, I can't even see the derned chart."

"Good! Excellent! There isn't one. Now, can you tell me the color of this tree?"

You can fool Hank the Cowdog once in a row or maybe twice in a row but not three times. "There's no tree, ma'am."

"There certainly IS a tree! This is the bottom part, called a root. It's brown. Yes, you have a problem, but I just happen to have a cure."

"You do?"

"I certainly do! Come over here, lie down, and hold still."

I did as she said. She closed her eyes and took the end of my nose in her claws. I watched her very carefully and memorized every step, and what you're about to hear is the secret combination that will cure Eye-Crosserosis. Here's what she said, word for word:

"Left, two." She twisted my nose twice to the left. "Right, three." She twisted it right three times. "Left, one . . . and push!"

I don't expect anyone to believe this, but it's the by George truth. When she pushed my nose, my tail shot up, my mouth fell open, and my eyes came uncrossed.

I told you you wouldn't believe it.

I could see again! Everything was clear! Madame Moonshine stepped back and smiled. "Oh, it worked! How nice! But to be sure, let's test it. How many legs do I have?"

"Two."

"Excellent! How many wings?"

"Uh . . . two?"

"Ver-ry good! Now just one last question. How do you expect to get out of here?"

"HUH? Well uh . . . I sort of thought you might lead me out and keep the snakes down, is sort of what I thought."

She shook her head. "Oh dear. You missed that one."

I glanced around and saw big Timothy coiled in the middle of my escape route. "What's the correct answer?"

She clapped her wings together. "The correct answer is that you'll stay and we'll play riddles—for days and days and weeks and weeks and years and years and ever and ever, until you solve one, and then," she shrugged, "I shall have to let you go."

"Now hold on. I've got a job."

"Rubbish."

"I've got responsibilities."

"Rubbish."

"I need to get back."

"Rubbish."

"And I'm gonna leave one way or . . ."

"Timothy?"

Big Tim started buzzing.

"On second thought, let's play riddles."

"Oh good! Here's one: if wishes were horses, beggars would be . . . what?"

"Uh . . . cowboys?"

"No."

"Saddles?"

"No."

"I really do need to get back, Madame Moonshine."

She laid down and propped her head up on her wing. "But you can't, Hank. I'm a witch and I can't stand for things to be simple. There must be a non-reason for everything. I can't just let you leave without a non-reason. No, you'll have to answer a riddle before I can let you go."

I studied Big Tim again. He flicked out his tongue. "Okay, let's hit the riddles."

"Here's a good one: How much wood could a wood-pecker chuck if a peckerwood's a checkerboard square?" I asked her to repeat it. "How much wood could a woodpecker chuck if a peckerwood's a checkerboard square?"

I said it over. "Can you give me a hint?"

"Just one hint. The answer's not what you think it is."

"That's a big help. Well, give me a minute. I'll have to do some figgering."

I had to use some algebra on this one. I mean, when you go to multiplying woodpeckers times peckerwoods and adding in all the chucks and chips and checkerboards, you've got to have some pretty stout mathematics. Plain old numbers won't work.

I figgered and I figgered. I wrote all my formulas in the dust, scratched out one or two, added a number here and a formula there, and finally came up with the answer.

Madame Moonshine was wearing a peculiar smile.

"Okay, here we are. The answer I get is 5.03."

The bottom fell out of her smile. "I don't believe it!" She sat up and stared at me. "No one has ever solved that riddle before! How did you do it?"

"Well, ma'am, all I can say is that they didn't make me Head of Ranch Security for nothing. I have certain talents, I guess."

"That," she said in a low voice, "is a monstrous understatement. You could very well be a genius!"

"You're not the first one that's said that, ma'am."

"I can imagine not!" She closed her eyes and clasped her wings together. "Oh dear, I shall have to let you go. Timothy? Open!''

The snake crawled over into a corner. Madame Moonshine sighed and led the way. On the way out, I could hear them snakes crawling around, and I was mighty glad Madame was leading the way.

When we reached the opening, I stepped outside. I looked around and I could see again!

"Well, Ma'am, I want to thank you for everything. You've done this ranch a tremendous favor, and we'll never forget it. Bye now.''

I trotted down the hill. "Oh Hank?'' she called. I stopped and turned back to her. "Do you believe in witches now?''

I had to chuckle at that. "Yes ma'am, I reckon I do. And do you believe in dogs now?''

She thought about that for a second. "No.'' And with that, she was gone.

Instead of going back to the ranch, I headed down the creek. I had a little errand to take care of on the next ranch.

WAR!

It was three miles to the ranch where Plato and Beulah and Rufus stayed. I kept to the creek for a mile or so and then got up on the county road when the creek made its big horseshoe bend to the north.

Boy, I felt good! The air was sweet with wildflowers and the sunshine warmed my back. My eyes worked, my aches and pains had gone away, and I could feel the muscles inside my skin, straining to get out and do hand-springs.

I made a mental note to myself: "Next time you get to feeling poorly, go see Madame Moonshine because she can cure more ills than Black Draught."

(I knew about Black Draught because Loper once used it to cure me of a case of worms.

Don't try it unless everything else has failed and it's come down to a choice between Black Draught and certain death.)

It was late afternoon when I reached the outbuildings of the ranch and by that time I had worked out my strategy. Instead of busting in and having a showdown right away, I would lurk around and check things out. Also give my highly conditioned body a chance to recharge.

I didn't want to underestimate the magnitude of the task before me. Taking on Rufus would be a handful, even on a good day.

I went creeping through some tall grass on the west edge of the place. I could see Billy down at the corrals, working with a young horse. Didn't see any signs of Beulah or Rufus.

I spotted a pile of old cedar posts and headed for it. I would set up a scout position there and just, you know, let the pot bubble for a while.

I reached the post pile and was peering around a corner when I heard a noise. Sounded like . . . it was kind of hard to describe, but it sounded a whole lot like teeth chattering. And it was coming from inside the pile. I cocked my head and listened.

"Who's in there?"

"Nobody," said a squeaky voice.

"Huh, you expect me to believe that? You ain't dealing with just any old slouch. You'd best come out before I get riled."

"Who are you?"

"Who I am is irrevelant. The order is for you to come out before I have to make kindling out of this post pile."

"Okay, I'm coming, but don't bite for Pete's sake, my skin tears very easily!"

Out came a spotted bird dog with rings around his eyes that made it appear that he was wearing glasses. He was trembling all over. You guessed it: Plato, my old rival in the love-of-Beulah department. We'd met once or twice before, but we weren't what you'd call bosom friends.

"Hank? Oh thank heaven it's you!"

"It may be too soon to thank heaven, Plato."

He slapped his paw against his cheek. "At first I thought you were that doberman. This has been an incredible experience. Would you believe five days in the post pile, I mean actually in fear of my *life*! I'm telling you, man, it's been . . ."

"Where's Rufus?"

Plato's eyes widened. "I don't know where

113

Rufus is, and that's okay. I've got nothing at all against the dog. I'm perfectly willing to relate to him . . . why do you ask?''

"I'm looking for him.''

"Good heavens! Why?''

"Grudge.''

"Grudge? Okay.'' He started backing toward the post pile. "Well, my position is very simple, Hank.''

"Your position better stay out of the post pile.''

"Sure, okay, but what I'm saying is that I don't really approve of grudges, the idea, I mean.''

"This ain't an idea.''

He nodded. "Okay.''

I peered around the edge of the post pile and studied the lay of the land. Then I caught sight of the enemy. He was down in the back yard, chewing on a big steak bone. Beulah sat a few feet away, watching him tear at the bone.

"Come here, Plato, and take a look.''

He crept over and peeked around the corner. "Good heavens! Just look at him!''

"Here's the way I figger it. You'll go down first and get his attention . . .''

"What!''

". . . and I'll move out and keep under

cover. While he's busy with you, I'll attack and hit him on the blind side."

"Wait a minute, Hank."

"I hate to take a cheap shot, but I got a feeling we're gonna need the element of surprise."

"Hey listen, Hank, I think we've got a basic misunderstanding here. What I have in mind is more of an advisory role, you see the distinction? I mean, I think my talents . . . listen, man, that dog is *terrible*! Do you have any idea what he can do with those teeth?"

"Got a real good idea, Plato. That's why I need a decoy."

"Decoy, is it? You mean a sitting duck. No way am I going down there to . . ." I turned on my slow rumble of a growl. Plato swallowed and blinked his eyes. "You're giving me no choice, is that it?"

"Yep."

"Suicide, that's what you're asking. Ho, what madness!" He began marching up and down in front of me. "You've spent years cultivating your mind, Plato, training yourself to hunt birds. Now all we ask is that you offer yourself to the dragon, to be torn into ribbons of quivering, bleeding flesh!"

"You finished?"

He stopped. "Yes, I am finished, in every sense of the word. However, if I might offer one small suggestion, suppose we held me in reserve . . ."

"Get going."

"Very well, all right, fine. But I must warn you: if I am maimed or disfigured, I shall hold you personally responsible."

"Hit the road."

"History will be your judge, Hank. Unborn generations of bird dogs will . . ."

I gave him a shove and got him out of there. I mean, he could have gone on yapping for the rest of the afternoon. I still had some work to do.

Rufus heard the commotion and looked up from his bone. He watched Plato walk down the hill, and a grin spread across his face. Beulah saw him too, and her mouth dropped open.

Rufus pushed himself up. "Ha ha! Fresh meat!"

"Listen, Rufus," yelled Plato, "I can explain everything. Try to control yourself for just a minute and hear me out. We've had a little misunderstanding here but I'm convinced that we can talk it over . . ."

"Watch my bone, honey." Rufus started

dragging his paws across the ground.

"Leave him alone, Rufus, he hasn't done anything!"

"He's alive, and I take that as a personal insult." He rolled his muscular shoulders and stepped out toward Plato.

The trap was set. I slipped away from the post pile and started creeping down the hill, taking cover behind shrubs and trash cans.

Plato started edging back toward the post pile. "We're in basic agreement on most issues, Rufus, except that . . ."

"I can't stand your face." Rufus was stalking him now, coming closer to the spot where I was waiting.

"Right, exactly, which is basically a superficial . . ."

All at once Rufus sprang into a lope. The muscles in his shoulders and thighs rippled. His teeth were bared and his little eyes glistened. All the world had narrowed down to Plato and that's all he could see.

I shot one last glance at Beulah, coiled my legs under me, and exploded out of the shrubs.

Plato stood on rubber legs and started babbling. ". . . can talk this thing out, Rufus, don't look at me that way, I can explain, don't tear my skin!"

G.L. Holmes

There's a kind of evil beauty about a doberman pincher who's moving in for the kill, a kind of gracefulness that sparkles when he's got murder on his mind. I caught a little glimpse of that, and then I hit him.

Old Rufus never saw me coming, never had the slightest notion that he'd wandered into my trap. I hit him with a full head of steam, which was important because I knew I'd have to stun him with a good lick or he'd come back and we don't need to go into that.

I put a real stunner on him, got a clamp on his neck and rode him to the ground. We rolled and kicked and snarled and ripped, sent up a big cloud of dust, tore up grass and weeds, and if I'm not mistaken, I think we even broke off a huge tree.

That gives you some idea of just how terrible a battle it was: I mean, things were flying through the air, the dust got so thick I could hardly breathe, tree limbs were falling to the ground.

Well, I gnawed on one of Rufus's ears and had things pretty muchly under control when, dern the luck, he put that same judo move on me, I should have been watching for it, got too preoccupied with the ear, and all at once he had me flat on the ground.

Then he hit right in the middle of me, kind of knocked the breath out of me.

I could hear Plato. "Sock him, Hank, knock his eye out! Give him one for me! Watch out, no no no, for Pete's sake, don't let him throw you, bad move, Hank, real poor move, you've got to keep the upper hand, use your teeth, man!"

"Get in here, you idiot, before he kills us

all!" I managed to holler.

Just then Beulah got there. Never thought I'd need the help of a damsel in distress; did though. She jumped astraddle his back and although she wasn't real big, she started reading him the riot act.

And then, to the surprise of heaven and earth and all God's wonderful creation, Plato hopped in. On a good day, he might be mean enough to chew up a wet Kleenex—maybe—but at least he was there and added a little weight to the pile. I was able to get one paw free and delivered a good stroke to Rufus's nose.

We got him on the ground and then playtime started. I was in the process of whupping the ever-living tar out of Roof-Roof when Billy came running down from the corral, yelling and waving his arms. His face was deep red.

"Hyah, get outa here! Hank, you sorry devil, go home!"

The rocks started flying. Plato and Beulah scattered for the post pile. I figgered I'd hang around for one more lick when I caught a stone in the upper back, hurt like the very dickens, and decided to evacuate.

I stepped off. "See you around, Roofie."

Billy chunked another rock that zinged past

my ear, so I loped up to the post pile.

"Don't you ever come back here!" Billy yelled. "Just let me get my gun . . ."

I ducked behind the posts. Beulah and Plato were there. She came up to me and nuzzled my chin. "You were just great, Hank!"

"Incredible, Hank, terrific job!"

They were right, of course, but you can't come out and say that. "Y'all didn't do so bad yourselves."

Beulah peeked around the corner and motioned for us to take a look. Billy was standing over his famous fighting dog and preaching him some hot gospel.

". . . two hundred bucks and then you get yourself whipped by a ten-ninety-five, flea-bitten, sewer-dipping cowdog!" (He was referring to me, by the way.) "I oughta just take you to town and find some other sucker . . ."

Never saw old Roof look so humble. Even them high-toned ears seemed a trifle wilted.

We held a little celebration there behind the post pile, then Beulah said, "You'd better go, Hank. Billy's mad enough to shoot you."

"When you're made of steel, you don't worry about lead."

Plato nodded. "Well put, Hank, very well put."

Beulah only smiled—that wonderful smile of hers that said, "You're probably one of the greatest dogs in the world and I'm about to fall helplessly in love with you but you'd better go," or something to that effect.

Anyway, she leaned up and kissed me on the cheek, which sent ripples of joy clean out to the end of my tail. "Goodbye, Hank."

So I loped off toward the creek and into the sunset. Just before I disappeared from sight, I stopped and gave 'em one last wave.

They waved back, which was fine and dandy, but when Plato lowered his paw, it came to rest on Beulah's shoulder. And instead of slugging him in the teeth, as she should have done, she let it stay there.

Moral #1: Time heals some wounds but makes others worse.

Moral #2: Women are hard to figger out.

Moral #3: Women are impossible to figger out.

Moral #4: Might as well give up trying.

CHAPTER

12

HOME AGAIN

It was dark by the time I got into familiar country again. Off to the north I could see the caprock brooding in the moonlight, and off to the south I could hear the bullfrogs croaking along the creek. Up ahead, I could see the dark outline of the machine shed.

I'd been gone for days and I had notched up some pretty exciting adventures, but it would be good to be back home again.

I wondered how tight the security had been in my absence. I had a pretty good idea, but I decided to give it a little test. Instead of coming into headquarters the back way, I marched right past the house and the machine shed, the vital center of the ranch operation.

No challenge, no warning, no order to halt, no barking, no nuthin'. I mean, the whole place was exposed like an open wound. Any scoundrel could have walked in there and had himself a picnic.

I went on down to the gas tanks to see if Drover, my assistant head of non-security, was pushing up Z's on his gunny sack. He wasn't there, so I moved on down to the corral. As I approached the saddle shed, I heard voices and slowed to a stealthy walk. I kept close to the fence and crept up to where I could see and hear.

"I'm tired of playing tag," said Pete.

"And I'm tired of chasing crickets. I kind of miss old Hank, don't you?"

Pete's head came up. "Hank. Now there's an idea."

Drover looked around. "Where?"

"Why don't we put on a play?"

"A play? What do you mean?"

"I'll be Hank and you be Rufus. We'll make it a comedy on Hankie."

"A comedy? You mean . . . we'll make fun of him?"

"Something like that." Pete flicked the end of his tail back and forth and rubbed against the post. "Now, wouldn't that be fun?"

"Well . . . it might be. But I bet Hank wouldn't appreciate it."

"Of course he would. You know what a wonderful sense of humor he has."

"I do?"

"Certainly! If he has a single fault, it's that he's always making jokes at his own expense."

"Hank does that?"

Pete went over and started waving his tail in front of Drover's eyes. The little mutt's head went back and forth in time with it. "And besides, Hankie's not around, remember? We can do *anything* we want, and what he doesn't know won't hurt him."

Drover glanced over his shoulder. "I don't know about that."

"Just watch the tail, Drover. Keep your eyes on the tip. That's better. Think of how much fun it would be." Pete was purring now. He brought the tip of his tail under Drover's chin and wound it around his nose.

"Maybe so. You don't think it would be . . . disrespectful, do you?"

"My heavens no! All you have to do is play Rufus. I'll do Hankie's lines. Just try to imagine that you're a doberman pincher."

"Well, all right . . . if you're sure . . . I just hope Hank doesn't catch us."

Pete rubbed on Drover's leg. "No one will be any the wiser. Now, make up your lines in

G.L.Holmes

verse and get into character. Here, watch me. I'll do the Hank-walk."

He puffed himself up and started swaggering around. Struck me as a real poor acting job. I mean, it was perfectly obvious that he wasn't imitating ME. What we had there was a classic example of how a dumb cat can play a dumb part and still come out looking dumb.

"And you see," said Pete, "I've got my eyes crossed and I'll start running into things."

Drover tried not to laugh. "That's not very nice . . . but it is kind of funny."

Pete ran into a post, grabbed his nose,

126

yowled, and rolled over on his back. "You're on, Rufus, say your lines."

Drover walked over to him, kind of stiff-legged, and here are the immortal words that came out of his mouth:

'My name is Roof and I've come with proof
That cowdogs are a silly invention.
Now get off the ground, let's go round
  and round
And chew on my bone of contention.'

Pete grinned and nodded. "Ver-ry good, ver-ry good! You're a blooming poet, Drover. Do some more, only this time make it a little . . ." He studied his claws. "*Nastier.*"

"Well, I don't know . . . I guess I could try . . . let's see here:

'I'm a doberman pincher and I don't wear
  dentures,
I'm big and I'm mean and I'm rude.
You think you're hot stuff, so get off your duff.
Hot stuff is my favorite food.'

"EX-cellent, excellent!" Pete tapped his paws together. "You're getting the hang of it now."

Drover gave a silly grin and wagged his stub tail. "You don't think it was too nasty, do you Pete?"

"It's only a play. It's not real."

"I guess you're right but . . ."

"Now it's time for my part. Enter Hankie."
Pete did his blind stagger routine again, puffed himself up and bounced off a couple of fenceposts:

'Sir Hankie's my name and protection's my
   game,
I usually stay angry and wroth.
I bet halitosis would beat crosserosis,
But dang it, I think I've got both!'

Drover covered his mouth with a paw but couldn't keep from laughing. "Oh, that's terrible, that's just . . . can you do some more?"

"You like that, hmmm? Give me a minute to think."

While he was thinking I figgered it might be a good time for me to say MY part. I had an idea it would bring down the house:

'My name is Drover, your little play's over,
Beware all you cats and dumb mutts.
You've had your good fun and now you'd best
   run
'Cause I'm fixing to start kicking butts!'

I stood up. All eyes were on me. Pete quit flicking his tail. "Hmmm. The cops are here."

Drover gasped and squeaked. "Oh my gosh . . . I knew we shouldn't . . . hi Hank . . . Pete made me . . . I told him . . ."

Pete started edging down the fence toward the feed barn. "Well, I think I'll do a little mouse patrol."

I turned on my incredible speed and in three jumps I had him rolled up into a hissing, spitting ball of fur. Drover started jumping up and down. "Git 'im, Hankie, git 'im!"

I gave the cat a pretty sound thrashing before he slipped out of my grip and made a dash for the feed barn. There's a hole at the bottom of the door, just big enough for a cat to slither through and not quite big enough for a dog.

Pete made a run for it, one step ahead of my jaws. He made it through the hole and I figgered, what the heck, I might as well tear the door down, so I lowered my head and rammed it into the hole.

Turned out the door was a little stouter than I'd thought, cricked up my neck pretty severely, and boy was I surprised when I couldn't get my head out of the hole. Had to throw everything into reverse and plow with all four paws before she popped free.

Drover was still hopping up and down. "Ata way, Hankie, nice work, boy we taught that cat!" I straightened my neck up and marched over to him. He quit hopping around and studied me. "Hank?" I kept marching, didn't say a word, and in a flash little Drover was highballing it up the hill to the machine shed.

I took out after him, figgered I'd catch him about half-way up the hill, only little Drover is faster than you might suppose when he knows his life's in danger. Never did catch the runt. He disappeared inside the machine shed.

"You might as well come out, Drover," I said, peering into the darkness and trying to decide which stack of junk he was hiding behind: the paint cans, the windmill parts, the old tires, the electric fence batteries, the spare parts for the stock trailer, High Loper's canoe, Sally May's wedding presents—you could have lost three elephants in that place. "Come on, Drover, and face the music. I see you."

"We was only funnin', Hank, it wasn't real. Pete said so."

"You coming out or do I have to tear this place apart?"

"I'm scared, Hank."

"Okay, you asked for it."

I waded in. When something got in my way, I just by George leveled it, knocked it aside, left it in rubble. You should have heard them paint cans clatter! I mean, when Hank the Cowdog gets on a case, nothing's safe, especially a villain. It's only a matter of time until I track him down and then you can imagine the terrible scene.

Drover was in real peril.

I tore the place apart, turned it upside-down, just about wore me out. "Drover, tell you what I'm gonna do. If you'll turn yourself in, we'll forget the death penalty. I'll let you off with a good thrashing."

"I'm still scared, Hank. I'm too scared to walk."

"All right, a minor thrashing."

"I'm just petrified, Hank, I can't move."

I thought for a long time. Justice has to be flexible. "Okay, here's my last offer. If you'll stand with your nose in the corner for fifteen minutes, we'll let it slide this time."

He came out. He'd been under the canoe. Sure thought he was behind the paint cans. "Now you march down to the gas tanks and put your nose in the corner."

"Okay, Hank, but that's a terrible punishment."

"You bet it is, and let this be a lesson to you."

We picked our way through the junk, across the cement floor to the door. When we got into the moonlight, Drover stopped. "Oh my gosh, Hank, look at you feet! You're bleeding!"

I glanced down. Sure 'nuff, my feet were covered with blood. Must have cut them on something sharp and terrible. I started getting faint from loss of blood. My legs got wobbly. "Rush me to the sewer, Drover, this is serious."

Drover sniffed the air. "Wait a minute. What's that I smell?"

Just before I lost consciousness, I sniffed the air. "Wait a minute. What's that I smell? It's paint, Drover, red paint. You saw something red and wet and jumped to conclusions. A lot of times you can study the clues, son, and figger these things out. Now march."

I marched him down to the gas tanks and stuck his nose in the corner. It was a terrible punishment, all right, but he had it coming.

Well, it was great to be home again. I mean, in just a few days' time, I'd managed to get all the loose ends tied together. I had my ranch back in order and things were running smoothly again.

Just to give you an idea of how well things worked out, around seven o'clock in the morning I looked up in the sky and saw the silver monster bird again, but he wasn't flying low this time, no siree, he was way the heck up there. I mean, you scare them birds bad enough and they'll stay off your ranch. They know the meaning of danger.

I was watching the monster bird pass over when I heard High Loper coming down the hill. I looked around and was shocked to see a smile on his face. And unless I was badly mistaken, he was even laughing to himself.

"Hank, by golly, I just heard the good news. Billy called, and boy, was he steamed up! Said you gave his doberman a licking. Heck of a deal, heck of a deal!" He whopped me on the side a couple of times, made me cough in fact, but that was okay. "This calls for a celebration. Double dog food, Hankie, come on boy, let's go up to the machine shed."

Off we went: a loyal, courageous dog and his master. It was just by George a pretty touching moment in ranch history.

But as you might expect, Drover tried to butt in—you know, as if *he* had done something to deserve special commendation, when in fact he was still on probation.

"You stay here, son, and think about doing right for a change."

Loper chuckled all the way up the hill. "Just

G.L. Holmes

went over there and whipped that old doberman, on his own ranch! I like that, Hank,
shows spunk and spirit and vinegar and . . ."

We had walked into the machine shed.
Loper stopped. His smile began to droop, then
it fell flat. The place was . . . well, a little
messy, shall we say.

His eyes went to the paint cans and the big
puddle of red on the floor. He looked at the
red tracks on the cement. He looked at my red
paws. I glanced around to cast an accusing eye

at Drover, but naturally the little dunce wasn't there.

I began to wag my tail.

I can't see that it would serve any purpose to go into details here. It should be clear by now that the machine shed was damaged in the line of duty. It should be clear that misunderstanding is just one of the prices of greatness.

Those of us who live on the heights must live with the judgments of small minds. We can only hope that in the next life justice will reign.

It reigns here, but it also hails.